WITCHES' CHILLERS

Night has fallen,
and magick is afoot . . .

The clock in the hall struck the hour, the chimes dancing through the air in an eerie melody. They began to chant, "Wild Hunt, Wild Hunt. Wild Hunt!" while Bethany took the yellow paper soaked in the Four Thieves Vinegar and lit it from the flame of the black candle. The paper exploded in her hand, sending sparks showering to the carpet. She didn't flinch.

The circle of her peers began to raise their hands, chanting louder and louder. Bethany joined in, her voice rising to fever pitch. They were consumed in their passion to find the killer, and they had become as one.

As if in slow motion she saw the picture window bellow, the moon's sharp visage warp, and then the explosion, shattering glass all around them.

Other Books by Silver RavenWolf

Nonfiction
To Ride a Silver Broomstick
To Stir a Magick Cauldron
To Light a Sacred Flame
Teen Witch: Wicca for the New Generation
Angels: Companions in Magick
American Magick: Charms, Spells, & Herbals
Halloween: Customs, Recipes, & Spells

Silver's Spells Series
Silver's Spells for Prosperity
Silver's Spells for Protection
Silver's Spells for Love (forthcoming)

Fiction
Beneath a Mountain Moon
Murder at Witches' Bluff (forthcoming)

Witches' Chillers Young Adult Fiction Series
Witches' Night of Fear (January 2001)

Kits
Rune Oracle (with Nigel Jackson)
Teen Witch Kit (forthcoming)

Visit Silver's website at
http://www.silverravenwolf.com

WITCHES' CHILLERS

Witches' Night Out

Silver RavenWolf

2000
Llewellyn Publications
St. Paul, MN 55164-0383, USA

This book is a work of fiction. Names, characters, places and incidents are products of the author's imagination or are used fictitiously. Any resemblance to actual events or locales or persons, living or dead, is entirely coincidental.

First Edition
First Printing, 2000

Cover art by Patrick Faricy/Mason Illustration
Cover design by William Merlin Cannon
Project management, book design and layout by Rebecca Zins

Library of Congress Cataloging-in-Publication Data
RavenWolf, Silver, 1956-
    Witches' Night Out / Silver RavenWolf.—1st ed.
        p.   cm.
    "Witches' Chillers."
    Summary: Bethany and the other members of her coven try to use the power of Wicca to solve the mystery of her boyfriend's death in a car accident.
    ISBN 1-56718-728-5
    [1. Witchcraft—Fiction.   2. Mystery and detective stories.]
I. Title.
PZ7.R19557 Wi2000
[Fic]—dc21   99-462288

Llewellyn Worldwide does not participate in, endorse, or have any authority or responsibility concerning private business transactions between our authors and the public.

All mail addressed to the author is forwarded but the publisher cannot, unless specifically instructed by the author, give out an address or phone number.

Llewellyn Publications
A Division of Llewellyn Worldwide, Ltd.
P.O. Box 64383, Dept. K728-5
St. Paul, MN 55164-0383
www.llewellyn.com

Printed in the United States of America

*This book is dedicated
to the 33 million teens in the U.S.A.*

You're all that—and more.

Chapter 1

Thursday, September 3

hate. She stroked the silky black fur of the cat nestled in her arms. The blades of the fan in her bedroom window spun a waft of sweet Indian-summer air across her brow, then slowed to a gentle stop. Satisfied, she watched the plump housekeeper walk across the grass, which was desperately in need of a final mowing. The woman looked like a white ship moving purposefully through the emerald green sea otherwise known as the Salem family lawn. A squawking crow circled the back yard, settling on the white picket fence, preening his glossy black feathers. The housekeeper continued toward her apartment over the garage. The woman walked with determination past the bird, ignoring his flapping wings and guttural squeal, her white clothing snapping in an afternoon gust. The fan whirred again, slowed, and stopped—just like life here in Cedar Crest.

Perhaps the bird would peck out the woman's eyes? Bethany Salem turned from the window. She wanted so very much to hate. But whom? Her father said it was just teenage angst. A lot he knew! All these months no one would listen to her. It was, "Poor Bethany. So terribly sad. You'll get over it."

She fingered the red leather collar around Hecate's neck. Bethany had no idea whom she should hate the most. Her father? The new housekeeper? The unknown creep who took Joe away from her? Or the friends who shunned her? There were so many people . . . One thing she did know. When she found the person that killed Joe, they would reap the bomb of hatred inside of her. They would rue the day they'd entered this incarnation. She would make sure of that!

Her tear-filled eyes skipped over the picture of Joe, the gilded frame capturing the pumpkin-gold light of the setting sun. He smiled back at her, frozen in time, suspended in her memory. Only a picture, after all.

The wreath crinkled at her touch. Stupid, she knew, to be so theatrical, fashioning the dried arrangement with its blood-lusting thorns and satiny black ribbons, then hanging it over—indeed almost obscuring—the picture of her dead boyfriend. With each twist of the ribbon, with each drop of her blood, she had willed the capture of the murderer.

That was three months ago.

Nothing had happened since.

Nada.

Zip.

Dead-ender.

Life in this stupid bedroom community of Cedar Crest oozed on as usual. She'd spent the summer doing normal stuff. Alone, but doing it anyway. The drive-in, swimming, horseback riding, golfing, the occasional trip to the amusement park, or an excursion into the Big Apple. Always alone, with the sporadic attention of her father, who forgot her sixteenth birthday. It was as if she had never existed. No one sent her a card or phoned with bright birthday messages. No presents. Nothing. She was a shadow in a busy world.

Today? The snapping point. It was the second day of school at Cedar Crest High. The halls filled with laughter but devoid of Joe's smile, his charismatic sweetness, his stupid jokes. She'd almost broken down and collapsed in front of everyone. Bethany's fingers toyed with the pentacle necklace dangling from the thin silver chain around her neck. Last year they'd had them specially designed: a pentacle surrounded by the eight phases of the moon. Each member of her group had one, though she doubted they wore them anymore. The silver disc grew warm in her fingers.

It wasn't like she had a lot to go on. Nobody believed her. But that was okay. She had a plan. Her idea coalesced over the summer, cooking slowly in her head, bubbling like a fine elixir in a Witch's cauldron, waiting until the thoughts aged enough to be plucked, refined, and put into action.

Today was the day.

And now she would begin. She knew she had to hurry. Some of them had already arrived. She heard the housekeeper let them in before the woman left. One thing more to do. With Hecate tucked uncomfortably under one arm, she withdrew a black votive candle from the dresser and placed the sweet-smelling candle in a glass cup. She lit the candle, murmuring the words her mother had taught her when she was a little girl. "Bright light, soul light, candlelight quickening. Shadows falling, I am calling, the strength of the Mother, the protection of the Father, the wisdom of Spirit. So mote it be."

Hecate struggled in her arms, emitting a low growl of discontent. Bethany scratched the cat under the chin, momentarily placating him. Whatever happened tonight, it would put things into motion that she knew she might not be able to control. But she didn't care—she hated, and that was enough. She was going to use her friends to get what she wanted. No guilt.

So, after school, she called them, and now, she knew, they were here.

The tears threatened to explode, making her eyelids feel thick, heavy, prickly. She swallowed hard. Mustn't break down now. Her arms clinched and the cat complained. Immediately she loosened her grip.

Laughter and giggles rose from the living room below, assaulting her ears. She once moved in the world of light. Now, she was changing and mutating with the world of shadow, where unsolved murderers went free and spirits like herself relentlessly hounded them. "To destiny!" she whispered at her large dark eyes that stared back from her dresser mirror. "To death!"

Slowly, she descended the stairs, the cat still in her arms, autopiloted by the voices of her supposed friends. People who refused to talk to her for weeks. People who called her crazy when she tried to get them to search for the truth. She was pleased that they had come. A small, darkly seductive smile touched her lips.

As she reached the landing, she heard Nick's voice, followed by Karen's. She glanced over her shoulder. Tillie's laughter echoed into the hallway. Nam answered a question. The cat fussed, arching his back to prove to her that he wanted down immediately. She let him go, watching him scurry back up the green carpeted staircase, his black tail rocketing to the ceiling. "Some familiar you are," she muttered, rubbing her arm to smooth away the surface scratches.

There was no sign of Ramona anywhere in the house. She'd seen the housekeeper leave from her bedroom window, but that didn't necessarily mean anything. Adults could be tricky. Especially this one. There was something sly about the woman, Bethany could feel it. Something not quite right. She flicked her thick hair behind her ears. The grandfather clock in the front hall chimed half past the hour.

In the beginning they called it Witches' Night Out, and the name stuck. They'd been meeting here, the six of them, at her house in secret. Every Thursday night for almost a year—until Joe's death. Until he never made it to circle. Until they found him dead on the highway, his head under the Route 15 sign, the rest of his body smeared along the gutter of Orr Bank Road—the car nothing but a poor excuse for safe American manufacturing.

A dead sardine had better protection.

She found her so-called friends in the family room. Her hand moved reflexively to her coven necklace. Would they be wearing their necklaces?

"Man, I thought that Ramona woman would never leave!" said Tillie, flopping down on the couch, lacing her brown fingers through the corn rows of her black hair. "How did your dad find her?"

Bethany tried to mask her feelings and smiled. "She just showed up at the door last week. Said she'd heard that our last housekeeper got married and moved to Arkansas. Weird." Bethany truly believed that somewhere in Tillie's gene pool there was fey blood. The Sidhe could be dangerous. It was those brown ears, pointed at the top, and the enchanted way she could guess whatever you were thinking. Definitely Old World fairy somewhere. Definitely a candidate who might enjoy killing.

Tillie rolled her golden-brown eyes. "The woman is odd!" she announced, smoothing the wrinkles from her scarlet skirt. Last year Tillie was into jeans.

This year she was into skirts and dresses.

My, how times do change.

Karen flipped her white-blonde ponytail with nail-bitten fingers. "And the way she talks about herself like she's two people . . . now that's psychologically unsound if you ask me!"

Nam tilted her head, blue-black shoulder length hair swishing across her blue velveteen jacket. Today the total color was blue. Nam always wore perfectly matching attire—blue jacket, blue blouse, blue nylons, blue shoes—blue, blue, blue. Tomorrow, the color may be pink, or green, or mauve. Her silver coven necklace shown brightly against the blue of her shirt. "It was like she was hanging around because she knew we wanted to do something. And that white clothing. What a strange fashion statement," Nam remarked. "Is she some sort of fanatic? What did you say her name was?"

"Ramona," replied Bethany, "as in moan." She clutched her stomach and imitated her best moaning sound. The others giggled. The pain in Bethany's heart receded, if only for a moment. "I made sure that Dad arranged her schedule so that she would have Thursday nights off. I thought she would never leave."

Nick stood in front of the picture window, his tall form illuminated by the September setting sun, his blonde hair ablaze with bits of orange-gold light. Joe's best friend. Team captain of the Cedar Crest football macho set. Rugged. The type of fellow who would mature into the world of dangerous outdoor sports. Interesting that he'd ignored Bethany when she tried to tell him at the funeral that something was wrong. Very wrong. Maybe he was involved.

Nick cocked his head. "She knows your dad is stuck at the precinct in New York City and won't be home until tomorrow. She said something about it when I got here. She probably thinks we're gonna take drugs," snorted Nick. "It took some smooth talking to get her to go."

"She probably thinks we're going to party," said Tillie as she threw her yellow Jordache backpack on the thick, brown carpet.

"Or drag race down main street," said Karen, giving an extra twist to her ponytail, making it look more like a dog toy than hair. She blinked her baby-blues and grinned. Did she have something to do with Joe's death? Bethany didn't think that her brain cells were capable of such a task, but you never knew.

Nam looked at the back of her small hand studiously, eyeing her blue nail polish. "Well, I kinda like this housekeeper. She's sort of . . . exotic, you know? All that white clothing against her olive skin. Like she came out of a movie or something. And I love her hair. All those thick plaits. Your last housekeeper was the pits!"

"Gone now," said Tillie, making an imaginary star in the air with snapping fingers.

Yes, thought Bethany, *and maybe it will be you who goes next.*

"I don't trust this Ramona woman. Where's she from, anyway?" asked Nick.

"New Orleans," said Nam, giggling.

"What's so funny?" asked Nick.

Tillie grimaced. "We only had to sit here and listen to her while Bethany was in her room. You were late, remember?"

"Like I told you when I got here, football practice ran late and then my sister asked me to run an errand for her. It took me longer than I thought it would."

"Which she probably had *planned*," said Karen. "Your sister is majorly crazy. Why don't you just chuck her away in a loony bin!"

"Let it go, Karen," said Tillie. "We've already talked about this before. Marissa hasn't gotten over," she glanced quickly at Nick, "the loss of her parents last winter. So she's a little overprotective. She'll come around. Marissa's just into that big sister thing right now."

Karen tossed her head, her ponytail zinging as if she'd been electrocuted. "I'm surprised she hasn't come to the door already, pretending that Nick forgot something just so she could check up on him," said Karen, shooting Nick a disgusted smirk. "It wouldn't be the first time."

"Gee, Karen, you're getting awfully vicious," said Bethany, holding up one hand in response to Karen's open mouth. "How would you feel if *your* parents died?"

"I wouldn't care," said Karen. "They're not the nicest people."

Bethany swallowed hard as the others stared at her. Tillie coughed. Nam let out a tiny, "Oh, dear."

"And all *you* can think about is your dead boyfriend," said Karen, turning on Bethany. "You've got to get on living. If you're not careful, you'll turn out like Marissa, crazy woman of the universe."

Horrid words threatened to explode from her mouth, but Bethany held on. Nobody paid the least bit of attention to her at the funeral. Her dad wouldn't even go with her. Too busy with his job and that bitch, Angela. He'd certainly forgotten all about Bethany's mother, cold in her grave in a town she'd only laid eyes on half a dozen times. And when Bethany asked him to look into Joe's accident, he said, "I can't, sweetie. Not my jurisdiction. Open and shut, anyway. I've got bigger problems to work on." Bethany curled her lip.

"Ramona's French Creole, I think," said Bethany, following up on the earlier thread of conversation. "Who cares? She won't last here, anyway. None of them ever do. I'm hoping when this one goes, Dad will realize I don't need a live-in keeper anymore."

Nam flattened her bubble-gum-pink lips. Thank goodness they weren't blue. "I don't know . . . there's something about her. She may surprise you, Bethany. You might like this one."

Tillie leaned back on the couch. "When it comes to getting rid of housekeepers, Bethany gives sweet sixteen a brand new meaning."

Bethany watched these so-called friends and listened to their conversation spiral about the room, gathering energy, funneling inevitably to a single conclusion. They were all trying to act like Joe wasn't a part of them. That he never existed. Bethany tightened her fingers in a reflexive motion. Well, she wasn't about to forget! She could feel the tension slithering underneath the laughter and the jokes. Joe was never coming back, and they knew it.

"I missed getting together on Thursday nights," said Nam, looking at the others. "Circle night always made me feel so good. When Joe died, well, I was afraid we weren't going to have another one. I'm so glad you called us all, Bethany."

For one tiny moment, Bethany felt a twinge of guilt. Could it be true? Had they waited all summer for her to make the first move? She looked at Karen's haughty expression and her hatred returned.

Nick ran his big hand over his chin. He had those chameleon eyes, the ones that change color depending upon his clothing or his mood. "So what are we going to do tonight?" he asked, looking at her oddly.

Bethany flicked her eyes away. "We're going to do a ritual to catch Joe's killer," said Bethany, her voice sounding clear and loud in the cozy room.

She could have heard a dust mote hit the bay window.

"I don't know, Bethany," said Karen uneasily. "I mean, it was an accident. Everybody knows that.

Why don't we do something else? I want to win the All-Star Cheerleader championship, can't we do something for that instead? Or maybe do something for the football team," she looked over at Nick, "so that we won't lose any more games?"

Tillie snickered.

"My father wants to bring our relatives over from China, but he doesn't have enough money. I'd like to do something for that," Nam said, a shy smile flitting across her mouth. "I thought we'd put this thing about Joe behind us."

"Your father not have enough money?" said Karen, a sarcastic edge to her voice. "That'll be the day!"

Nam lowered her green eyes, her lower lip trembling, her little hands stiffening into claws. "It takes a lot of money to bring five people into this country. Not only will he pay for my brother and sister, but there are my grandparents and a cousin whose parents were killed in Tiananmen Square."

Tillie cleared her throat. "My dad doesn't like the church he's ministering at. He thinks they're too stuffy. He'd like to build his own church, one for all faiths, but he doesn't have the money or the backing. I was hoping we could do something for him tonight." She reached beneath the collar of her shirt and pulled out her coven necklace. It twinkled as she adjusted the silver chain, the eight phases of the moon almost alive on the disc.

Bethany could feel her rage building, but it would be too dangerous to let it go just yet. "When we started Witches' Night Out, we agreed that we would work for whatever each one of us needed," she said slowly. "We've done spells and rituals for healing sick people, for getting good grades, for finding Tillie a familiar, and all sorts of stuff. In all that time I've never really asked for anything special. I'm asking you tonight, please, I want to do a ritual to find Joe's killer."

"Yeah, and tomorrow a dead Joe will end up on your doorstep," said Karen. "He was driving too fast during a terrible rainstorm. He lost control of the car. He hit a telephone pole. That's it. Joe killed Joe. I vote we do magick for the football team."

Chapter 2

Nam's soft voice circled the room. "I think we should do the ritual for Joe. Even if it doesn't work, it will make Bethany feel better and she's always helped us when we asked her to." Her blue clothing reflected onto her pale chin, making Nam look like a doll-like corpse rather than a living, breathing human being.

Tillie paced the room, snapping her fingers. "Okay. That's two yes votes. How about you, Nick?"

Bethany held her breath.

Nick hesitated, looking from Karen to Bethany. "Joe was my best friend. I think it was a legitimate accident, but if there's a chance that someone hurt him on purpose, then I think we should do the ritual, too. We can do the other stuff next week." He pulled his coven necklace out of his pocket and put it on. "Can't wear it during sports," he said sheepishly. "I don't want to lose it."

"That's three yes votes," said Tillie. "What about you, Karen?"

"I don't like it and I didn't bring that stupid necklace. I think I lost it."

"Karen votes no," said Tillie, throwing Karen a

dirty look. "Even if I do vote no, Karen, you're out-numbered. Therefore, the ritual is a go."

Karen let out an exaggerated sigh. "I guess that means that the football team will lose again tomorrow night. If this was my group, we wouldn't even think about doing this stupid ritual and we wouldn't be parading those necklaces all over the place either. People might see them, and then how would we explain it?"

Tillie flexed her fingers by her sides. "We all know that the fate of the football team rests on your shoulders, Karen, but the last time I checked, all have an equal say here. Or has that somehow changed in the last twenty-four hours?" Her grating voice sunk through them like cleats on hot tar. "I didn't realize that you didn't want to stand up for your religion—that your popularity is far more important than we are."

There was a stunned silence. Bethany held out her hands, fingers extended and trembling slightly. This was working out better than she'd hoped. "Okay. Okay. We're all upset. We're all frustrated. Joe's . . . ," she swallowed, "death"—there, she'd said it, hard like the last boom in a fireworks display—"may have been an accident, but as a member of Witches' Night Out, he deserves the best we could give him—and that's finding out the truth. It won't do us any good if we fight with each other. Remember the rule, none of us can enter a magick circle if we're angry at each other. Karen doesn't have to wear the necklace if she doesn't want to. Some people feel they need to stay in the closet for a lot of reasons. We don't have any right to judge their choices."

Karen crossed her arms over her chest, attempting, Bethany thought, to shield herself. "The papers said he was like a human oil slick." Karen punched a pillow. "This is ridiculous," she snapped, her ponytail whistling through the air as she jerked her head back and forth. "We could tell if he'd been murdered. We're Witches! Besides, if it's somebody we know, we'd already know it . . . right?" Her eyes flicked frantically around the room at the others. "Right?"

Tillie, dark eyes like old blood with glowing flames, put her hands on her hips. "Really? How?"

Karen's eyebrows dipped and her nose wrinkled. "Well. Um. I just thought . . . I mean we are . . . like, magickal people . . . right? We should be able to tell these things."

"We may be magickal people," said Bethany carefully, "but we're not God and none of us are all that experienced. I mean, everything we've done so far has worked but none of us have ever tried to catch a killer before." And one of you knows who did it, she though silently. I *know* you do.

"You know, Karen," said Tillie, "I think somebody pulled that ponytail of yours too tight and cut off the circulation to your brain. Only people in books have that kind of power. Did you think we could just point and zap?" she asked, jutting out her hip and flicking her wrist in the air, snapping her fingers in the shape of a pentacle. "Get real, girl! All those winning cheerleading competitions have gone to your head!"

Karen dropped her chin, her jaw flexing beneath the creamy skin. "We've been practicing Witchcraft together for about a year. Almost every week we hold circle, um, up until Joe's death, anyway. All of us have spent a lot of time studying. If we were being stalked, we would *know*. We may not be the most experienced people in the world, but we're not new at this, either."

The muted chimes of the grandfather clock in the front hall struck the hour.

Bethany hesitated. So far, only Karen was putting up a fuss. Maybe she'd been wrong. Maybe these people really *were* her friends, but just didn't know how to handle her odd behavior these past few months. No. She had to find out. "We'd better not waste any more time," she said.

The picture window presented nothing but the misty dark blue-violet of the deepening September dusk. If Bethany squinted she could make out the charcoal outline of a few trees, blazing fall foliage scratching the sky, leaves highlighted for just a moment by the flood of silvery streetlight.

Nam wiped her eyes with the back of her hand. "We should do a divination first. You know, to check to see if we should do this at all."

"Waste of time," said Karen. "We should just go ahead and do it. Joe's dead. D-E-A-D. Gone. This is just a major waste of time."

Tillie drummed her hands on the floor. "No! We should check first. If we're too impatient, we could really mess this up. I agree with Nam. The divination, then the ritual."

"Okay," said Karen, a sneer curling her lip. "Let Nam do her little divination. We'll finish putting the stuff together. Maybe if we get this over with fast enough, we can work for my cheerleading competition."

Nam fished a small brown pouch out of her purse, closed her eyes, and began shaking it. The stones inside clicked lightly together as she shook the pouch. "Should we perform this ritual tonight?" she asked softly, sliding her eyes around the room to make sure everyone had heard her.

They all waited. Perfectly still.

"Stop doing that!" said Nam. "You're making me nervous. I can't concentrate with everyone watching me."

The family room walls seemed to vibrate with something special. Something strange. Magick was afoot. Bethany could feel it. Her fingers were already tingling. Yeah, this was the right thing to do . . . if she could pull this off. She hoped so. She could hear the clicking of the stones in Nam's bag. Nam hadn't chosen one yet. Bethany wished she'd just get it over with.

Hecate, Bethany's black cat, slithered into the room, avoided the commotion in the center, edged around the baseboard and jumped lightly onto the wide ledge beneath the picture window. Bethany smiled and thought of art class—"Cat Framed by Autumn Sunset While Witches Prepare to Catch Killer."

Tillie poured Four Thieves Vinegar over a piece of yellow paper, then flapped the paper to force the drying time. "For truth," she said.

And still the stones in Nam's pouch clicked.

Hecate jumped from the ledge and slithered around Nick's jean-clad legs. He picked the cat up and scratched him under the chin. Hecate's purr sounded like cake pans banging together in a hot, steamy kitchen.

Tillie looked at Bethany. "Did you check the astrological almanac?"

"The moon is moving into Scorpio," she answered, "which means whatever we do will be way intense, especially since she's full. The astrological sign of Scorpio is good for issues concerning death, taxes, intense passion, revealing secrets, and law enforcement." She looked out the picture window at the blackening sky. "I don't know what more we can do to make it right."

Nick put the cat down. Hecate made miffed kitty sounds. Nick ignored him. The cat stalked over to the couch, did a double jump and hung over plush sofa back, his tail twitching.

The stones continued to click together in Nam's small hand. Click, click, click. Nam still had not chosen a stone.

Bethany bit back a comment to make her hurry up and turned her gaze to the picture window opposite the doorway. The full moon hung low and heavy, suspended like a rotten orange in the black heavens. This was supposed to be such a cool Halloween. All six of them were going to drive out to the beach and do their Samhain celebration there.

But not any more.

Not without Joe.

"White!" shouted Nam and all heads turned in her direction. "We proceed!" Her face was flushed and victorious, those green eyes of hers looking unnatural, like those of a haunted doll. Bethany had a momentary flash of uneasiness but, like the others, she was caught up in the anticipation of what they were about to do. Only Tillie looked pensive.

"I hope we've done everything right," said Karen. "I don't want a dead Joe banging at my door. My parents would have a fit!"

Tillie shivered. "Reminds me of a book I read for English class. The author always writes 'had I but known' and then proceeds to tell you how everybody gets offed."

Bethany watched their shadows dance against the walls in the flickering candlelight. The full moon shone directly in the center of the circle, where the black candle's elongated flame shot into the air with broiled determination, ebony smoke spiraling from its very tip. The heady scent of the incense filled her nostrils and for a moment she swayed, her spirit reaching the still point where all cares are released and the universe is but a dance of harmonic light. She forgot Joe was dead. She forgot about the stares she got in school. She forgot about the endless nights of crying. For a brief moment, she forgot who she was. No father who ignored her. No crazy housekeeper. No one making fun of her because she was such a tomboy. No one telling her she was crazy because she knew Joe had been murdered.

The five of them stood in a circle, holding their coven necklaces and breathing in unison. Karen, her face unreadable, let her hands hang at her sides, her gaze stuck to the floor. Finally, they held hands and began the sequences necessary to become a group mind, each doing their part, unmindful of the time since they'd last met. Even Karen fell easily into her tasks.

The ritual halfway completed, the time of raising power had come. Bethany blinked. She couldn't remember anything from the last ten minutes but they must have done it right so far, or she would recall, right? The others were looking at her expectantly.

Hecate skittered through the circle with his ram-rod-straight tail. He yowled so loudly it reminded Bethany of a baby's scream. Nam jumped, gripping Bethany's hand and cutting off her circulation.

"Psycho cat," muttered Tillie. The others laughed nervously.

Bethany broke Nam's grip and moved to the center of the circle. Nick quickly grabbed Nam's shaking hand, closing the circle around Bethany. The sensation of expectancy stole over her, laced with determination and power. She faced the picture window so that she could see the moon clearly. She could feel her lips pull back into a slow, canine grin as she raised her arms in a sensuous, graceful gesture, her palms pointed at the full moon before her. She took a deep breath. *I was born for this,* she thought. *I can do anything!*

"Dark Mother, Queen of the ghostways, I call thee!" cried Bethany. "Great Mother, She who protects Her hidden children, come now into our circle and aid us in this rite!"

The others replied, "So mote it be."

The quarter candles sputtered, the flames spitting, rising, falling . . .

"Be with us this night!" called Bethany.

The incense boiled in the censer, sending clouds of heavy fragrance spinning around her head. She was not controlled by the environment, she had command of it.

"We stand between the worlds in a place of power and safety," said Bethany. "The Wheel of Life and Death, Birth and Surrender moves within our lives. The seasons pull our Mother from bloom to full power, to the gentle slumber of gestation and rebirth. Sweet Mother, with your gown of ebony, sweep your heavy skirts of destiny. We implore you, great Mother, send the Hounds of the Wild Hunt to find Joe's killer!"

Tillie's eyes widened and her mouth dropped. "Oh, Bethany," she murmured. "I'm not sure you want to do that . . ."

The clock in the hall struck the hour, the chimes dancing through the air in an eerie melody. They began to chant, "Wild Hunt. Wild Hunt. Wild Hunt!" while Bethany took the yellow paper soaked in the Four Thieves Vinegar and lit it from the flame of the black candle. The paper exploded in her hand, sending sparks showering to the carpet. She didn't flinch. The circle of her peers began to raise their hands, chanting louder and louder. Bethany joined in, her voice rising to fever pitch. They were consumed in their passion to find the killer, and they had become as one. As if in slow motion she saw the picture window bellow, the moon's sharp visage warp, and then the explosion, shattering glass all around them.

Nam screamed and shrunk to her knees, her dark hair spilling over her face. Tillie growled, her hands shooting up in front of her to grab whatever necessary. Nick stepped forward, saying, "What the—?" while Karen tumbled to the right, her white ponytail lancing through the air. Bethany remained standing in the center, never feeling the bits of glass as they bit into her flesh, staring at the strangest thing she thought she'd ever seen: Ramona swatting someone over the head with a broom.

Repeatedly.

She felt the heat first, the blaze seconds after. Her eyes dropped to her feet, her mind trying to comprehend that the cauldron with the black candle had flown off the altar, spraying bits of hot wax in several directions. The rich, deep carpet sizzled, filling her nose with a disgusting smell. The bottle of Four Thieves Vinegar lay broken at her feet, the liquid ignited by the candle flame. Tillie rushed forward, snatching up the candle. Karen screamed, more out of anger than fear, and stomped on the carpet with her sneakered feet, while Nam regained her senses and doused the flames with the holy water from the altar.

"Oh, man . . . ," said Tillie, looking first at the mess and then out the window. Ramona's strong dusky-olive arm was wrapped securely around what looked to be a young woman with blonde hair. No match for Ramona, the figure struggled, uttering strange, animal sounds. Ramona proceeded to drag the woman out of view, presumably toward the front of the house.

"I don't believe this is happening," muttered Tillie. "Who *is* that?"

Glass crunched as Karen scurried around the room, dousing the remaining candles and grabbing at the general disorder. Nam jammed as much as possible in the ritual box while Nick threw open the family room door and bounded out into the living room, followed by Tillie and Bethany.

"Call police! *Allant!* Go!" shouted Ramona, dragging the bedraggled woman into the living room. "Ramona says, call them *maintenant!* Now! I caught this piece of garbage peeping in the window, and then, big as she pleases, she picks up a stone and she throws it and breaks the window!" Ramona shoved the woman onto the living room floor. Beads of sweat ran down the housekeeper's plump cheeks, her white clothing flapping in soiled disarray. "Ramona says, get on the phone! What's the matter with all of you?"

Bethany's mouth dropped open, not sure if the woman with the bleeding scalp and matted hair was who she thought she was.

The woman tried to crawl away, but Ramona would have none of that. She stuck her foot square onto her back and pushed. The human mess in front of them went down with a whumph.

Nick rushed to the young woman's side. "Don't do that! It's my sister!"

"What?" said Ramona, her black eyes wide. "*Mais, no!*"

Bethany couldn't believe it. It *was* Nick's sister! "Marissa! What did you think you were doing?" She looked wildly at Nam and Karen as they entered the room, their mouths open in shock. Karen was the first to recover, her eyes slitting and her chin up. If hatred was a physical thing, it was slithering around

Karen. Bethany knew the feeling well.

Marissa raised her head, her lips curling. "I'm going to sue your father, Bethany Salem, for everything he owns." She grabbed Nick's necklace and tried to rip the pentacle off his neck but the chain refused to break. Her fingers slid off the chain, leaving a surface slice on her skin. She yowled.

Nick stepped back, dropping his sister's arm. A thin thread of blood trickled down his neck. "What are you saying? Why would you do such a thing?"

"Corruption of a minor," she spat, raising herself slowly to her feet, brushing her torn skirt and flipping her matted hair out of her eyes. "I told you these people were no good, and with what I saw tonight I have enough information to break up this little gaggle of degenerates. Go ahead and call the police! I'm going to tell all of your parents what you've been doing here! You're not going to twist my brother's mind. You and your little cult!"

Bethany could feel the group mind solidifying, merging around her. She didn't have to see their faces or hear their voices.

"Did you hear me?" demanded Marissa, looking straight at Bethany. "You're done for, you and your sick little group! It was your fault Joe died. I know it! It's all your fault, Bethany Salem!" she screamed, pointing a bloody finger at Bethany.

"Joe's death was an accident!" Karen walked right up to Marissa, sticking her nose in the woman's face. "You've been a nutcase for months. Everyone knows it. You lost your job. My mother said so. Said you're so crazy nobody will speak to you anymore. You even talk to yourself when you eat at the diner. You're a loser. Los-er!" She splayed her fingers in the shape of an L.

Marissa's face turned white with rage.

"Look what you've done to Bethany!" squealed Nam.

Bethany glanced down at her arms and hands. Where had all that blood come from? At the thought of it, the cuts began to sting and her anger grew. "Was it you?" she asked Marissa, with a cold edge to her voice. "Did *you* kill him?"

Marissa took a tentative step back, but Ramona grabbed her roughly by the shoulder. "No, n-no," stammered Marissa. "I would never hurt . . ." her voice trailed as she looked at Bethany. Only the ticking of the clock in the hall broke the eerie silence.

Ramona turned to Nam. "Ramona says, call police. Now. You. Tillie, is it? Take Bethany upstairs and clean her up." She turned a fearsome gaze on Marissa. "You! Sit on that chair until the police come. If you move, I'll deck you, sure as the saints know I'm standing here. I don't know what it is with you Northern people," she said in disgust. "I was reading a good mystery, quiet as you please in my own apartment, when I look down into the yard and see this thing," she pointed a shaking brown finger at Marissa, "snooping around. Ramona doesn't like to be disturbed when she is reading. *Especially* when

I'm at the good part." She began muttering in French.

Hecate padded into the room, swinging his amber gaze from Ramona to Marissa. Apparently satisfied that things were under control, he stalked out to the kitchen.

Tillie dragged Bethany up the carpeted steps to the bathroom. "I don't *believe* you called the Hounds of the Wild Hunt," she hissed. "You realize that if there isn't a real killer, they'll turn on us? And now, since you didn't direct them, they'll be hanging around here! They may not even be able to get the killer. Unless circumstances are right, we're liable to be the ones gobbled up. Who knows when they'll strike? You should have told me when you called me this afternoon what you wanted to do. You sure better hope that all this isn't a figment of your imagination or we're in deep crap!"

From somewhere over the small hill behind the house came an unearthly howl. Tillie's eyes widened. Bethany shivered. *What have I done?*

Chapter 3

Friday, September 4

Nam picked at the solidifying macaroni on her plate. "I can't believe Ramona lied for us," she said softly, her delicate voice wavering. "Why would she do that?"

Bethany guiltily crunched on a carrot stick. She wished she hadn't dragged Nam into this, but if she hadn't called all of them, the others would have been suspicious. "I have no idea," she answered, shoving the unhappy thought to the back of her mind. "But the cops sure believed her."

Nam leaned forward. Today she was dressed entirely in yellow, right down to her shoes. Bethany wondered if she color-coordinated her underwear too, not that it was any of her business. "When Ramona told them that we were all watching a movie in the family room and that she was there with us the whole time, I thought I would just die!"

The Cedar Crest High lunch room continued to fill, the chatter of over a hundred and fifty students almost deafening. Bethany took a sip of her chocolate milk, ignoring the stares of the other kids.

29

"Guess my face looks pretty bad, huh?"

"You're a good candidate for a used pin cushion," said Tillie. "Does it hurt?"

"Very funny," replied Bethany. "It stings more than anything else."

Nam cracked a sunny smile, matching her outfit. "It doesn't look that bad, really."

"Yeah. Right." Bethany rolled her eyes. "I can't understand what happened. Marissa shouldn't have been able to see what we were doing if we'd cast the circle the right way."

Karen sat back and crossed her arms. "Actually, she didn't see much of anything. She was zonked on drugs from her psychiatrist. When the cops looked at all the pills she had on her—well, that was the end of the story," she said. "I talked to Nick this morning before I left for school. One of the reasons why the cops believed Ramona is because Marissa wasn't making any sense and didn't have any real information to give them. Besides, with Bethany's dad being a cop, who'd you think they'd believe?"

Tillie ran her tongue over the top of a butterscotch cake. "So, where's Nick?"

"He's home with his sister. They sedated her, said she's going through some sort of trauma episode." She shrugged. "I personally don't care if she drops dead, but she certainly got what she wanted—Nick by her side. It's sick, if you ask me," Karen continued. "Child services isn't coming in because Nick turned eighteen last week. I hope they permanently hospitalize her," she said, her words influencing the energy around the table with a waspish sting.

Nam flicked her dark bangs out of her eyes. "That's not fair," replied Nam. "It's obvious she's in a lot of emotional pain."

Karen shrugged her shoulders. "There's lots of people in pain and they don't behave like that. I think it's all an act. Homecoming is only a week away and all I can say is that woman better have one heck of a fast recovery!"

Tillie attacked a second cake. "What did your dad say, Bethany? I bet he was mad!"

Bethany grimaced, the cuts on her face sending messages of discomfort to her brain. "I haven't talked to him. Ramona said he called this morning. He must not be too upset because he told her he'd be away for another few days," said Bethany. "Figures. Someone breaks into our house, but he's too busy with other, more important crimes."

Nam shook her raven tresses away from her face. "And Ramona didn't say anything else?"

"Nope. Well, yes, she told me to eat my oatmeal and not be late for school. She was cooking something noxious on the stove when I left. I'm sure she'll tell him the whole story when he gets home. He's her paycheck, after all."

Nam said something just as the din around them rose when a few boys at the other end of the table started a food fight. Bethany shook her head and leaned closer to Nam. "What did you say?"

"Do you think we did something wrong in the ritual last night?" yelled Nam.

Bethany selected another carrot from her brown bag lunch and chewed thoughtfully, not looking at Tillie. "I don't think so," she shouted back, watching a glob of macaroni hit the principal, Mr. Kuhn, directly between the eyes. Good. He deserved it. He was such a tyrant. "It felt okay," she said lamely, "at least until Marissa messed it up. You did say that the divination supported the ritual, right?"

The boys at the end of the table scrambled out of the lunch room followed by a raging Mr. Kuhn. Nam's expression made Bethany nervous, for though Nam's words indicated that yes, she chose the white stone, those emerald-green eyes said something different.

Tillie twirled a carrot in her hand. "I still think, though," she looked pointedly at Bethany, "we shouldn't have used the Hounds of the Wild Hunt."

Nam wadded up a bunch of dirty napkins from the table, her green eyes wide. "Why not?"

Tillie's jaw hardened, but there was an impish light in her sooty eyes. "Because if they don't catch who you send them after, they come back after you!"

Karen flicked her white ponytail with a cuticle-reddened finger. "You're not serious. What a bunch of malarkey."

Tillie cocked her head, a small smile playing across her lips. "I'm *deadly* serious."

Karen trilled, "What a major psycho drama! You guys are *way* too intense. As if such a thing exists. Where'd you find this out? On the Internet? In some dumb book?"

"Unlike you," Tillie sneered, "I actually *do* research. Don't you get it yet, Karen? This isn't a *game*. It's not a *joke*. The Craft carries a lot of power within its teachings. We may have made a real mistake here. If Joe's accident was just that, an accident, then there is *no* killer—*no one* walking around to take the blame. If those ethereal hounds cannot find their prey, WE will become the prey." She grabbed Karen's ponytail and jerked her head. "Do you *understand* me?"

"Hey! You're hurting me," pouted Karen, trying to delicately extricate her hair from Tillie's grasp. "This whole thing is just a farce anyway," she said shakily. "We're just in it for kicks. So our spells work. So it just proves the power of the mind."

"And *you* were the one who thought that because we called ourselves Witches, we would know if someone was a killer?" asked Tillie, a hard light frothing from her dark eyes as she let go of Karen's ponytail. "So this has all been a *gag* to you? Whose side are you on, anyway? I'm telling you that if we did anything wrong in that ritual . . . Any. Little. Thing . . . we could all be in very big trouble!"

Nam let out a little "Oh! Oh, no!"

"What's the problem?" asked Tillie tersely, shooting a hard look at Nam.

Nam opened her mouth to answer, her eyes wide and frightened, but the lunchroom intercom system crackled to life, cutting off her reply. "Will Bethany Salem, Tillie Alexander, Nam Chu, and Karen Wolf please report to the office," said the echoing feminine nasal voice. "I repeat, will . . ."

Bethany looked at the others. "What's that all about?"

Mr. Kuhn sat at his desk, sweating profusely and wheezing, bits of macaroni still stuck to his tie. "I'll get right down to the point," he said, wiping the perspiration from his flabby neck with a yellowed handkerchief. "I have it from the highest authority that you young ladies are involved in some sort of Satanic group and I'm informing you that I want this nonsense to stop immediately. I have called your parents and I've instituted a three-day suspension for each of you until we can sort this out."

He held up his fat hand as all four of them began to protest. "There is nothing you can say at the moment to convince me otherwise. Your lockers have been searched. We have the evidence we need. He held up several books on Wicca, a baggie filled with green leaves, and worst of all, a dagger that Bethany immediately recognized as belonging to Joe. Frantically she tried to figure out where those things came from. None of them kept anything in their lockers because of the mandatory searches done every month.

"You are to wait in the detention area until your parents come to take you home," said Mr. Kuhn, a haughty smile playing along his corpulent lips. "You know, I've been waiting for the opportunity to boot you misfits out of here. Looks like my wish has been granted. That's *my* kind of magic." An ugly, piggy sound issued from behind his bad teeth.

A brisk wind danced across the parking lot, rattling the chain link fence that caught dead leaves like a metal spider's web. A sob hitched in Bethany's chest. They'd taken them away. First Nam's parents—angry, abusive words enclosing Nam in a cocoon of tears. Then Karen's mom, tight-lipped, white-faced, latching on to her ponytail and forcing her into the pickup truck. Tillie's father said nothing. He just stared at the both of them, then turned on his heel. Tillie followed meekly behind. *I'm the last one,* thought Bethany. *There's nobody to come for me.*

All I had was Joe.

And he's dead.

Bethany wished she'd worn a sweater or jacket this morning, and wrapped her arms around herself, shivering as the wind bit into her flesh and cut at her eyes. School actually let out an hour ago and she'd had to sit on the concrete bench outside the front doors as just about the entire school trooped past her and called her names like Satanist and Baby Killer. It was revolting. How could this be happening to her—to all of them? Who would have been mean enough to do this? This isn't what she'd intended at all. She felt so guilty. Her hatred had done this. Her magick had created this.

She tucked her heavy hair behind her ears. Maybe one of the circle members had done this. Karen? No, she was in just as much trouble as the rest of them. Nick? He wasn't here today. Somehow she felt that Nick couldn't have done this. He wasn't in trouble though, was he? The old anger boiled within her, tightening her shoulders, pressing at her temples.

"Doesn't seem fair, does it, *mon cherie?*" asked Ramona.

Bethany looked up, startled. "Do you own any color other than white?" asked Bethany peevishly.

"And don't be taking your bad luck out on me," spouted Ramona.

"Why not?" asked Bethany, anger sending the blood rushing to her temples. "You told them. You're the only one that could've."

Ramona shook her head. "*Jamais!* Never! Ramona didn't tell nobody. No sir, not me. People's magick is their own business, but these Northern folk, they won't understand. Pack of stuffy hyenas, if you ask me." She waved her hand toward the glass doors of the school, where Mr. Kuhn peered out at them, a smirk playing across his bloated lips. "Like that fella in there. No mind. Absolutely no brains about him. Wife probably dominates him at home so he has to come here to work out his petty problems on impressionable kids." She snapped her fingers and a big gust of wind pounded the glass doors. Mr. Kuhn jumped back as if he'd been bitten. Bethany raised her eyebrows. Ramona laughed. "Small minds scare easy, that's for sure. *Bouffon!* Fool! Come on. We got to get you home. You know, you got a lot to tell your daddy."

Bethany chewed on her lower lip. "What did you say to him?"

"Not what I told him," said Ramona, lifting up Bethany's backpack and slinging it over one white shawled shoulder. "It's what you're gonna tell him. He'll be home tomorrow night. He's bringing an attorney with him."

"You mean he's bringing Angela home with him. Convenient," spat Bethany. Angela Davis had the hots for her dad. That female viper would use this as an excuse to play up to Bethany and win points. Bethany knew it was all a joke. Angela didn't care about her at all, but Bethany wasn't about to tell Ramona anything. After all, just because she said she didn't tell the school didn't mean that she'd really kept her mouth shut. They walked in silence through the deserted parking lot, the autumn air cloying in Bethany's nose. Bethany's cherry red Camaro sat alone. She'd thought about just getting in and driving off earlier, but she feared bringing more grief down on her head.

There wasn't another car or truck in sight. "How did you get here?" asked Bethany, looking at the vast expanse of empty macadam.

"Ramona *marcher*. I walked," said Ramona, throwing the backpack into the trunk.

Bethany turned in surprise. "You walked? It's over twelve miles from here to the house!"

"Don't I know it," said Ramona, getting in the front seat and kicking off her white shoes. "I was reading a thriller when I got the phone call. I was right at the good part! Next time you plan to get in trouble, do it closer to home."

Bethany started the car, the familiar smooth hum of the engine soothing her nerves. "Why didn't you drive the sedan dad left you?"

"You needed time to think. Did you use it wisely, or did you sit there and feel sorry for yourself the whole time?"

Bethany threw the car in drive and gunned out of the parking lot, tears welling in her eyes. First the loss of Joe, then that mess last night with Marissa, and she'd been suspended from school and now her father was bringing the Beast of the East home to roost and, on top of it all, she had to deal with a snotty housekeeper. What more could go wrong?

Ramona threw her a sidelong glance as she took the turn onto Orr Bank Road a little too hard. "By the way," she said. "When your papa hired me, he didn't say nothing about four big black *chiens*—dogs."

Bethany was concentrating so hard on herself that she didn't quite understand the woman. "What do you mean?"

"The big black dogs in the backyard. Ramona is not taking care of any dogs. You'll have to do it."

Bethany gripped the steering wheel. "We don't have any dogs, Ramona. Only the cat."

"Humph!" was all Ramona said. "Some cat. He thinks he's human. Like I said," she looked at Bethany, sending chills up her arms, "I'm not taking care of no dogs."

Chapter 4

Saturday, September 5

*T*illie's voice floated through the receiver of the telephone. "You've been fired," she said, "and so has Nam."

Bethany gripped the phone, collapsing on her bed. "What are you talking about?"

"Nam just called me. Seems Karen's mother went ballistic. She fired both of you from the diner. You're to turn in your uniforms. She wanted Nam to call you, but her parents only let her make one phone call."

"Sounds like jail," said Bethany, panic seizing her brain. She'd never be able to make her car payments without that job. What was she going to do? Bethany collapsed onto her bed, stuffing her head into the soft goose-down pillows, compliments of an L. L. Bean buying frenzy by one of her father's old girl-friends. "This can't be happening to me," she said in a muffled voice, the phone clutched tightly to her ear.

"You'd better believe it, girlfriend," replied Tillie. "And it gets worse."

"How could it possibly be worse?"

"Nam's parents have transferred her to a private school, that's how worse."

Bethany sat up, her heart pounding. "Oh, no! Poor Nam! What are we going to do?"

"Beats me," said Tillie. "I knew it was a bad idea to do that ritual. You know, she confessed that she lied about the divination. The stone was really black, meaning we shouldn't have done it."

"Nam? Lied?"

"She did it because she thought it was what you wanted her to do."

Bethany did not reply, she couldn't find the right words. Instead she ran her free hand back and forth over the red, orange, and gold patchwork quilt beneath her, fingertips playing over the raised stitching, her hand moving in and out of the bright bands of morning sunlight streaming through her bedroom window. Yesterday she didn't care who got hurt. Today, she wasn't so sure. Those guilty feelings circled around her head like a halo of bloodsucking bats. She shivered. Tillie always had that uncanny way of knowing how a person felt. Bethany shoved her feelings deep down inside of herself. After all, Tillie could be the killer. Was Tillie right? Did Bethany really have that much influence over her friends? Enough to make them lie to please her? She didn't like that thought. Not at all.

"Since you're not talking, I'll assume you're thinking the same thing," said Tillie. "So now what do we do?"

"Some rituals can take thirty days to play out. I just wanted to draw out the killer. To do to him or her what they've done to Joe's family. And to me. I never meant to hurt Nam."

"No, but our lives are certainly breaking apart into tiny pieces," snapped Tillie.

Bethany tried to change the subject. "Have you heard from Karen or Nick?"

Silence. Finally, "Not a peep."

Bethany picked at a stray thread on the quilt. "None of this is making sense. We've been into the new school year what—two, three days? Who would know about Witches' Night Out? Even better, who would really care? I just don't understand this."

Tillie coughed. "I don't know. I've been thinking about who put that stuff in our lockers, and what they found in whose locker. Some of those things belonged to Joe. Who but one of us would have been able to get that stuff, and how did they get it in our lockers?"

"We've had those lockers since we were freshmen," said Bethany. "Anyone could have figured out our combinations in the past two years."

"That doesn't answer the who question," replied Tillie. "Or do you think Ramona told?"

"She says she didn't. I don't know why, but I think I believe her. I mean, what's in it for her if she said something? Besides, she covered for us. Why would she turn around and blow the whole thing? She could have easily said something when the police were here."

"Maybe she didn't want you to get in that kind of trouble," said Tillie.

"There's something else . . . it's probably nothing. I'm really not sure if I should say anything or not . . ."

"I'm listening . . ."

Bethany looked at the picture of Joe on her dresser. He smiled at her. That same cute, sexy grin. She swallowed hard. "Ramona claims that we have four big black dogs in the backyard."

"What? No way!"

"I think she just saw some of the neighbors' dogs. They don't enforce the leash law around here like they should." Bethany flopped on her back. "You didn't really mean what you said about the Wild Hunt, did you? Where did you hear that?"

Tillie didn't answer.

"You don't trust me, do you, Tillie?" asked Bethany.

A pause. "It's you who doesn't trust me."

Bethany immediately switched the course of the conversation. "So what did your parents say?" Tillie had hit too close to home.

"Actually, not much. I thought they'd pray over me or throw holy water at me, but they didn't. They said that if it was Witchcraft I was practicing, that they knew about that. My dad even said he understood that it was a nonharmful, earth-based religion; however, he's upset because he says his congregation probably won't understand and he may be forced to find a new job."

Bethany groaned.

"Mom said that she doesn't like most of the women at the church anyway. They're snobs. She said maybe this was the perfect time for my father to get off his behind and get that church together that he's been talking about. I never realized that adults would make such a big deal out of an alternative religion. I never meant for my dad to lose his job. I just didn't think people could be so dumb. Basically, they're hurt that I didn't talk to them about it more than anything else." Her breath came out in a sad whoosh over the receiver.

"Don't sigh, Tillie, it will work out okay," said Bethany, feeling more guilty than ever. But why should she, on second thought? None of these people, including Tillie, had called her all summer long. They'd left her hanging in her own misery. Whatever they got, they deserved.

"My parents are sitting right here," said Tillie.

"You mean they know you are talking to me?" asked Bethany.

"Sure. In fact, my dad suggested I call you. He says he'll talk to your father if you need him to. Is your dad home yet?"

Bethany pounded her free hand listlessly on the bed. "He got home late last night. He brought Angela with him. I haven't spoken to them yet. I faked I was asleep."

It was Tillie's turn to groan. "Not the Beast from the East?"

The muffled chimes of the grandfather clock in the hall on the first floor echoed through the house. "How are we going to get out of this mess?" asked Bethany.

"I don't know," said Tillie. "We'll manage somehow."

Bethany sat in the family room on the sofa, hands folded primly in her lap. She'd taken special care to wear the clothes she knew her father approved of and applied her makeup lightly. Better to look young and innocent. The pale blue sky beyond the newly installed picture window looked somehow foreign, as if it didn't belong to the planet she was currently trapped on. The trees in the backyard drooped with listless, faded color. They matched her father's current expression.

Hecate stared out the window, fascinated when a dead leaf would spiraled up on a brief puff of wind, skittering across the glistening pane. Quick black paws batted the glass, to no avail. The clock in the hall ticked ominously. Bethany dug her bare toes into the new forest-green carpet, compliments of Ramona's speedy arrangements.

"Ramona says, one should always walk on the color of prosperity and healing," whispered Ramona while it was being installed last night. Of course, the fact that the family room carpet now matched the carpet in the hall and living room had nothing to do with the choice.

Mr. Salem and Angela stood looking at Bethany like she was a nasty viral infection. Bethany shifted uncomfortably, her palms sweating.

Angela spoke first. Tall Angela. Lithe Angela. Angela, the beautiful adult, focusing on Bethany, the ugly progeny of her father. "They simply don't have a case," she droned coolly.

Angela the Ice Queen. "Witchcraft is a legal religion in the United States these days, and is even acknowledged by the military service. I have a copy of the U.S. Army's chaplain handbook in my briefcase to prove it." Her gray eyes glinted like bits of brittle, dirty ice. "I'll have them groveling by this evening, but you shouldn't be messing in things you don't understand, Bethany, and you should have told your father about your interests. Look at all the trouble you've caused for yourself and your friends. Your father had to take time off his job to come home and take care of your muddle," she fingered the heavy gold earring on her right ear. "It appears that new housekeeper of yours can't keep you out of trouble. You should be ashamed of yourself!"

Angela the Wicked.

Bethany looked at the carpet, her jaw tightly clinched. "Don't lecture me," she said in a quiet, deadly whisper. "You're not my mother."

Bethany's father stepped forward, deep shadows feathering into the deep wrinkles under his eyes. He looked so tired. "Bethany, please. Angela is only trying to help you."

"I can do without her help, thank you very much."

"Bethany!" he said. "I've brought you up to behave better than this!"

"You brought me up to treat people decently if they act the same way to me. This broad," she pointed at the glamorous Angela, "doesn't have a shred of morality in her. She's a lawyer! A shark. A leech. A person who gets rich sucking off other people! Wake up, dad, she only wants the money mom left you. You don't really think she's fallen for someone like you!"

Her father curled his fists, clenching his fingers tightly, pain searing his eyes. Bethany immediately felt guilty. Why had she said that? Hurting her father was the last thing she wanted to do. Or was it? Did he look a little grayer at the temples? Was his premature aging her fault? Bethany was so mad she didn't really care. The nerve, bringing the Beast of the East into this house—her mother's house!

Angela simply raised her eyebrows and smiled demurely.

Bethany wanted to slap that feline grin right off her face. Angela the Perfect.

"It's all right, Carl," said Angela, grinding a delicate, black high heel sharply into the new carpet. "She's only a teenager. Hormones. Infantile behavior," she waved five expensively manicured fingers in the air.

They looked like she'd dipped them in glistening crimson blood. Bethany's blood. Right from her jugular . . .

"She's just being normal. You look exhausted, Carl," she purred. "Why don't you go upstairs and get some rest? I'll handle the school. I've called a special meeting with their legal counsel. Bethany can stay here and do whatever teens do." She waved that manicured hand at Bethany as if she was flicking a fly off the sofa. "This just goes to show my point last night. The girl needs to be in a special school where she'll be watched twenty-four hours. There are lovely schools in upper New York. I urge you to reconsider."

Angela the Terrible.

Bethany could not believe what she was hearing. Angela was talking about her as if she wasn't there. As if she was a pet to be kenneled when the owners got bored of it.

"Maybe you're right," said Carl Salem, not looking at Bethany. "Perhaps I was too hasty in turning your suggestion down, but right now, I just can't think properly. Are you sure you don't need me to go with you to that meeting?"

"Not at all," said Angela. "Not at all. You know, Bethany, your mother wouldn't have approved of your behavior," she added, her tone sickly sweet.

"You never met my mother!" shouted Bethany. "She was a kind and wonderful woman and she would roll over in her grave if she thought my father had taken up with trash like you!" Tears burned against her eyelids.

"Bethany!" shouted her father.

Ramona stepped forward from the shadows. "*Pardonne moi*. Pardon me. Mother and daughter the same."

How that woman could sneak around the house all dressed in white, Bethany could not fathom, nor did she expect Ramona to speak in her defense. The Beast of the East did not look pleased, thinking the battle lines were clearly drawn. Bethany could see the woman's mind working. Ramona added a new element to the mix. Angela's eyelids narrowed.

Angela extended her soft hand to Ramona, who ignored it. "I'm Angela Davis. You must be the new housekeeper." She played with an earring, as if she hadn't noticed Ramona's snub.

"I'm the keeper," said Ramona, abruptly turning her back on Angela. "Bethany, lunch is ready. On the kitchen table. You go eat. Mr. Salem, I've set a place for you and the lady in the dining room. You should eat and then lay down to rest. *Manger*. Eat." She waved her plump hand toward the dining room.

Angela emitted an odd little laugh as Bethany's father followed Ramona like a trained puppy. The Beast from the East turned on her high heel, and whispered to Bethany, "I'll get you out of this mess, you little brat, only because it will help my reputation and make me that much more endearing to your father. I suggest that you learn to stay out of my way."

Angela turned a gold band around on her left ring finger, exposing a vibrant tear-shaped diamond. "Oh, and just to inform you. Your father proposed to me last night, so you can deep-six any idea of getting rid of me. It is *I* who will be disposing of *you*."

Bethany pounded up the staircase as fast as her feet would carry her. All she could feel was rage. Rage, rage, rage. Pulsing red rage. Screaming black rage. She heard glass breaking in the dining room below but she didn't care. Maybe the Beast of the East ran into the French doors and slit her throat.

It couldn't happen to a nicer person.

Chapter 5

Angela's artificially blushed cheeks glowed with victory as she entered the hallway. The clock boomed five strokes. Mr. Kuhn, she informed them, was properly decimated, and was now on the unemployment line. Her eyes glittered like a thousand light-enhanced swords. Her honey-poison mouth gleamed like the jaws of a shark after its first taste of blood. Bethany thought that if she drew a pentacle on the floor and snapped her fingers three times, the demon Angela could possibly manifest.

As much as Bethany didn't care for Angela, she certainly didn't feel sorry for that jerk of a principal. He deserved whatever he got. On the other end of the broomstick, now she had to deal with this very same Angela who was going after her father just like any other legal case. Systematically, Angela the Conqueror was plotting to reap the benefits of making nice for Bethany, which would lead to Bethany's mommy's estate. Bethany wanted to gag.

"Don't you want to congratulate me?" asked Angela, reaching for a water glass at the dining room table over dinner, her long nails clicking sensuously against the Waterford crystal.

Ramona shoved a cheap tumbler in Angela's hand, saying, "To save the good crystal. *Plastique.*"

Angela shot her a devastating look. "I already apologized for breaking the glass this afternoon."

"Fine," said Ramona, holding her ground. "*Plastique.*"

"Really, Carl, are you sure that woman is working out?" whispered Angela loudly, turning her body slightly away from the housekeeper.

Bethany's father looked a little better, but Bethany wasn't sure if that was because they were eating by candlelight or not. "I like her," Bethany said, realizing what she'd just admitted. *Me? Like a housekeeper? Never!* But it was too late, the words were out. Ramona smiled, her white form gliding silently back to the kitchen.

Mr. Salem cleared his throat. "She came highly recommended. Bethany says she likes the woman. Is there something wrong?"

Bethany watched the exchange gleefully. Dad had his cop eyes on tonight. He always got that piercing look when he felt things coming together on a case. She hoped he was seeing clearly now, but just as quickly the glance passed and he patted Angela's hand lovingly. "I'm sure you'll like her. Besides, she'll be here with Bethany while we're in the city. Both of our careers are very demanding. We need someone here."

Angela was not ready to let it go. "Bethany is sixteen now. She doesn't need a nanny."

Bethany was all for her own independence. Heck, she'd managed to destroy the sanity factor of at least ten nannies and even more housekeepers, but this crafty Angela was gearing up to send her away from the only home she'd ever known, her friends, and worst of all, her father. "I would prefer that she stay right now, Daddy," said Bethany, trying to put a soulful expression on her face. "With Joe's . . . uh . . . accident (the word was hard to say), and then this mess at school . . . well . . . I mean . . . can she stay, please? At least for a little while?"

Hecate stalked into the dining room, winding his black, sinewy body in and out of the chair rungs. Bethany slipped him a piece of chicken.

"Of course she can," he replied. "Angela, would you please pass the mashed potatoes? This woman's cooking is marvelous!"

Angela tried to throw Bethany a slicing glance, but Bethany purposefully bit into a fat leg of fried chicken, so huge that it obscured her vision.

Angela dabbed her mouth with a snowy napkin. "There is one concession I had to make today, Carl. I hope you don't mind. I agreed that Bethany would go into a brief psychiatric program. It won't be anything drastic," she said quickly. "But with the death of her mother, then her friend, and the fact that she's an only child and you're not around much . . . well, it would be good for her."

Bethany almost choked on her chicken. Hecate sat patiently by Bethany's chair, waiting for another morsel of chicken.

A horrible crashing sound emanated from the kitchen, ending with a crescendo of something falling, like numerous pans, to the ceramic tile floor, followed by a tirade of French. Hecate jumped, skittering under the table. That cop look returned to her father's eyes, making Bethany's hopes soar, but just as quickly he looked at the beautiful Angela. Angela the Child-eater. His steady gaze disappeared as she watched him melt back into the hussy's vile clutches.

There had to be a way of getting rid of this woman. There just had to! She heard Hecate hiss. Bethany quickly peered under the table, just in time to see Angela's spiked heel munch purposefully onto Hecate's tail. The cat yowled, hissed, and slashed Angela's creamy ankle. *Next time, kitty,* she thought, *aim a little higher. Like her carotid artery.*

"I have the perfect doctor," said Angela breezily. "Excellent man. I've been using him for years in court cases."

Carl Salem sat back uneasily in his chair, that hooded look back in his eye. "I don't know, Angela. I'm not comfortable with a stranger talking to Bethany simply because someone in the school system is uneducated and acts on fear. I know all about court-appointed physicians. There are good psychologists involved with the police department. If it is absolutely necessary, I'll make the arrangements, and you can advise the school system of that point."

Angela's pretty face momentarily twisted. "Really, Carl," she said, toying with her earring. "I certainly wouldn't send her to someone that I didn't feel was highly qualified."

Her father smiled and patted her hand. "I'm sure you wouldn't . . ."

Bethany held her breath. Would her father cave in?

He shook his head. "However, I stand firm on this one. You understand."

Angela smiled demurely, but her eyes glittered deadly cold.

"Maybe we could just turn her into a toad," said Tillie, glancing through a teen magazine. "You know, like point and zap, something like that." She flipped a glossy page, munching on a fistful of popcorn.

It was Saturday night, and her father and Angela the Temperamental had gone to a local theatre production. Bethany stirred her hand listlessly in the bowl of buttery popcorn.

"That's only in the movies, silly," said Nam, stroking Hecate's black fur. He wore a satisfied cat grin—given that cats could grin, of course—and perfectly matched Nam's outfit for today, black on black, including black lipstick and fingernail polish. After Angela's pit bull legal mojo, Nam's parents decided that she didn't have to attend private school and that Bethany wasn't the devil's spawn. Both Tillie's and Nam's parents were joining Angela's civil suit against the school. She had to admit, Angela had performed miracles in only a few hours. The fact that both of her friends were allowed to come over and visit was a testament to that!

Karen's parents, however, had not been so quick to respond. Angela wanted to sue them too, as Karen's mother did fire Nam and Bethany from the diner, but the girls were able to convince her not to hurt their friend.

Thank the Goddess for small favors.

The three girls sat on the floor in Bethany's bedroom. "My father's talking about going back to the city tomorrow," said Bethany, choosing a nail polish from the tray in front of her. "Angela is still lobbying to send me away to school, some place in upper New York State called the Savannah something-or-other, but Dad says that if he makes that decision, it will be after they are married."

"Is he taking Beast of the East with him back to the city?" asked Tillie.

Bethany shook the bottle vigorously. "I'm not sure. She says she wants to stay until Monday and take me to that psychiatrist, but one of her cases got spicy, so she postponed the visit until next week. I'm not happy about that at all. She could tell this psychiatrist anything and he'd believe her."

"You know," said Nam, looking thoughtfully out the window. "We could bind her . . ."

Tillie grinned. "Not a bad idea! Let's do it!"

Bethany, all interest lost in the nail polish, seriously considered the idea. Regretfully, she said,

"Binding something holds the energy to you. I don't want the Beast of the East stuck in my life."

Nam sighed, pushing her raven-black bangs out of her eyes. "I thought it was a good idea, but if you put it that way . . ."

"Where did your father meet this tramp, anyway?" asked Tillie, popping another fistful of popcorn in her mouth. A few pieces dropped into the nail polish tray. Bethany brushed them out.

"I don't know," said Bethany. "He never told me. I assume working on a case."

"Those blouses she wears are real silk," observed Nam. "And those suits? They're straight from a Fifth Avenue couturier. She has very expensive taste."

Tillie picked up another magazine. "I still vote we turn her into a toad."

Nam giggled and started chanting, "Toad, toad, toad, toad, may the powers that be find the road, turning Angela into a toad!"

Tillie joined in. Bethany couldn't help herself. She chanted, too, until they all fell on the floor, giggling, spilling the bowl of popcorn.

A chilling howl rose from underneath Bethany's window.

"What was that?" asked Nam, a laugh caught in her throat, the soft light of the bedroom bouncing off her emerald-green eyes making her look like a cat caught raiding the trash. The black turtleneck she was wearing just added to her slinky appearance.

"Probably just the neighbor's dog," said Bethany, walking over to the window. Tillie followed her, but Nam hung back.

"Look down there!" said Tillie, pointing at four black shapes that seemed to float across the lawn. "What's that?"

Bethany shivered, the hairs on the back of her neck curling. She opened the curtain wider to get a better view. "Like I said, probably just loose dogs."

Tillie threw her a sidelong glance that said, 'Oh, yeah? I don't think so.'

"Bethany?" asked Nam.

Bethany felt a tickle of irritation. "What?"

"Where'd you get that picture of Joe over your dresser?"

Bethany dropped her hands from the curtain, turning to face Nam. "Why?" she asked, her tone of voice edgy, like bad dragon's breath.

"Sorry," said Nam, her green eyes misting like wet bits of jade beneath a heavenly waterfall. "I . . . I just wanted to know because it's not like any school picture I've ever seen."

Bethany shifted her weight uncomfortably. The picture was the source of her argument with Joe, which was the last time she'd spoken to him the night he died. He'd handed it to her before he got in his car. "Keep this safe," he'd said. "This way, I can always smile at you."

She really didn't want to talk about it. "It was taken for the New York Times. Some photographer.

About his scholarship."

"Oh," said Nam. "It's a nice picture," she said, her voice soft and hesitant. "But the wreath. Well. It's sort of scary." Those green eyes searched Bethany's face as of to ask what the black candle was for. Nam touched the rim of the candle cup. She quickly withdrew her hand as if she'd been bitten. "Very scary," she whispered.

"Yeah," replied Bethany, drifting away from the window, "it should be."

Tillie stared at Bethany, a frown creating a deep wrinkle across her smooth forehead.

Bethany could feel her friend mentally digging into her mind. She turned away.

"Now for some breakfast. Ramona makes the best fried bananas," announced Ramona, bustling around the cozy kitchen.

Bethany glared at her under sleepy eyelids. How dare this woman be perky on a Sunday morning? She slumped into a kitchen chair, rubbing the grit out of her eyes. She looked around, her vision trying to adjust to the harsh morning sun streaming through the kitchen window, blinding bands of light bouncing off the toaster and the microwave. She squinted and turned slightly to avoid the glare. The countertop was cluttered with all sorts of herbs, a mortar and pestle, and several small amber bottles, as well as the peels of several small, weird-colored bananas.

"*Bien!* Good!" said Ramona. "You'll see. Okay, okay, I'll make bacon and eggs, too."

"What's that junk on the counter?" asked Bethany. "Looks like you bought out an apothecary. Whipping up a little poison? Be sure to give some to Angela."

Bethany's father sauntered into the kitchen. "Something smells wonderful!" he said, sniffing the air and rubbing his chin.

"Fried bananas!" said Ramona, with a hint of pride.

Carl Salem wrinkled his nose, then grinned. "If they taste anything like that dinner last night, I won't complain."

Ramona bowed at the compliment, her white, billowing clothing swishing in the warm kitchen air.

Angela stepped into the kitchen. The atmosphere immediately changed from warm to polar. "Good morning, everyone!" said Angela brightly, the light from the window glinting on her gold earrings. She stopped dead, the color draining from her face. She took another step, a smaller one this time, and again she stopped.

Carl Salem looked up at her, his brow furrowing. "Is something wrong, Angela?"

Angela batted her eyelashes. "No. Of course not." She stepped forward, pulling hesitantly on one of her big, gold earrings. And stopped. "I just . . . I don't know. Do you mind terribly if we eat in the dining room?"

Bethany's father seemed reluctant to leave the kitchen, but finally he said, "I suppose we could. I just thought that the kitchen was more . . . homey." He tussled Bethany's hair, making her giggle.

Angela smiled, but the smile didn't reach those sewer-gray eyes. "I just thought that the child and the help might wish to eat alone."

Angela the Swamp Creature.

"Can't you stay in here, Dad? It would be like old times," said Bethany, trying to control the hurt that threatened to strangle the words coming out of her throat. And what was that mark on Angela's cheek? Did she drip some of her makeup?

Angela appeared to be frozen in place. What, by the power of the Morrigan, was wrong with the woman? Hecate sauntered into the kitchen, sat at Angela's feet, and promptly coughed up a hairball.

Angela screamed in mortification. "If it is all the same, I'd rather eat in the dining room," she said stiffly, now clenching her fists at her sides.

Ramona cleaned up the mess. Bethany could hardly control her laughter, but she picked up the cat, fearing Angela might kick it with one of those deadly spiked heels. Today they were cream, to match her neatly tailored suit. What was that about white after Labor Day?

Again Bethany watched that cop look flash into her dad's eyes but, again, the expression receded as she heard him say, "Certainly, if that's what you want." Bethany closed her eyes as her father stood, then walked closer to Angela. "What's that on your face?" he asked her.

Angela's hand flew to her cheek. "Oh, why, I noticed it this morning. I don't know what it is. I don't remember it being there yesterday." She threw a sidelong look at Bethany, who eyed her with growing curiosity.

Carl Salem delicately touched Angela's cheek. "It looks like . . . well . . . a wart."

"No!" exclaimed Angela, drawing her head back in dismay. "It couldn't be!" She ran from the room, with Carl Salem in panicked pursuit.

"I'm sure it's nothing," he called after her. "Just sit down here in the dining room. We'll have breakfast and then on our way into the city you can call your dermatologist."

"It's not fair," Bethany whispered. "It's just not fair!"

"That's one bad woman," muttered Ramona. "She's got a coat of evil on her like the sweaty film on an oiled bodybuilder."

Bethany laughed. She couldn't help it.

"Toads and warts," mused Ramona, looking at Bethany oddly. "They do go together. So they say."

"So they say," echoed Bethany.

"*La femme monstre!*" muttered Ramona.

Chapter 6

Slamming her locker, Bethany hurried to join Tillie and the others in the gym, where they planned to decorate for the Homecoming Dance tomorrow night. She ran a cool hand over her face. The cuts from the glass had just about healed.

The members of Witches' Night Out spent a quiet but socially void week at Cedar Crest High. Although Bethany called, no one wanted to come to circle on Thursday evening. Shades of the past summer, she thought sadly to herself. No one at school went out of their way to talk to them, except to make a few nasty comments.

"All bullies look for the weak spot," Ramona said this morning, as Bethany ran around frantically trying to find her letter vest she'd earned last year from the Cedar Crest hockey team. "Don't show them one."

Always an outcast except on the hockey field, Bethany still felt the pressure of the entire student body of Cedar Crest closing in on her. Or maybe it was just her imagination.

And still, she waited for Joe's killer to appear.

At least she hadn't heard those stupid dogs outside of her window since last Saturday night.

One of the preps, Vanessa Peters, cut her off, edging Bethany toward a blind corner in the hall.

"Hey!" said Bethany, a little irritated. "What's the problem?"

"You are," sneered Vanessa, chomping on blue bubble gum. "You know, it's all over school. We don't want any devil worshippers at Cedar Crest." The bubble gum peeked from between her lips, reminding Bethany of iridescent barf. Vanessa sucked in the blue goo with a slurp. "Why don't you and your lame little friends get out now, before something bad happens. You know, Mr. Kuhn is my uncle."

Bethany sucked in her breath. A void settled in her stomach.

"Yeah. I'm going to do something about you people." She cracked the gum. "Me and my friends. We won't put up with your kind of trash in our town."

Bethany raised her chin. "Like what do you think you can do?"

Vanessa's eyes appeared colorless, sort of like the hue of doom. She coyly picked at Bethany's shoulder-length hair with golden nails, her jaw muscles playing with the gum. "Oh, you know . . . ," she said, wrapping her fingers tightly into Bethany's hair and pulling just enough to hurt, but not enough to tear the hair.

Realization struck. "*You* put that stuff in our lockers! How did you get Joe's ritual dagger?"

Vanessa cocked her head, her mouth slack showing the blue gum mixed with saliva, her thinly plucked eyebrows raised in a "so what?" peak. She cracked her gum and smiled.

Instinctively, Bethany pushed Vanessa away, feeling that familiar power surge from her solar plexus, into her arm and through her fingertips. Too late, she realized she'd pushed too hard. Vanessa stumbled backward, still gripping Bethany's hair, teetered, then sprawled on the high-sheen linoleum floor, her backpack spilling its contents, the blue gum flying from her mouth, and long strands of Bethany's thick hair wrapped around her golden fingertips.

It took a moment for Vanessa to realize most her body had tumbled to the floor. Her expression went from shock to anger to a frenzy of tears. "I'll get you for this, Bethany Salem, you just wait and see!" she cried, smudging her tear-soaked makeup with the back of her shaking hand, then raising a fist at Bethany, brown hair still clinging to her hand.

"Buzz off," spat Bethany, trying to rein in her anger. So much had happened in the last few days, she just wanted to jump on top of Vanessa and beat the snot out of her, but she knew that would be morally wrong. Just one tiny punch? Bethany shook her head, trying to control her emotions. Thank the Goddess she wasn't carrying her hockey stick or she was sure she'd start to use Vanessa as a hockey puck. Send her clear into the net. Yes, she would! In desperation, Bethany turned on her booted heel and stalked down the corridor. She could hear Vanessa shouting her name mixed with obscenities, like an echo from a bottomless cavern. Bethany never looked back. She knew if she did, she'd rush back and kill the little fool.

Karen looked at Bethany. "What's with you?"

Shaking, Bethany sat down on the bleachers. "Vanessa Peters threatened me, can you believe that? I have a new name for her: Vanessa the Viper."

Karen twisted her head vehemently, her white-blonde ponytail almost laser slapping her rosy cheeks. "You're kidding! Why would she do that?"

The back of Bethany's neck prickled. Karen's demeanor seemed sincere, but those too-blue eyes were not. The last time she'd felt this way, Nam had lied about the divination.

Bethany took a deep breath. Sometimes she wished that her observation wasn't so keen. "Vanessa threatened all of us. Called us devil worshippers."

Karen put a sneakered foot on the bleachers and leaned toward Bethany. "I talked to Tillie and Nam. How come you didn't invite me over to your house last Saturday night?"

"I thought your mother wouldn't let you come. I mean, she fired Nam and me from the diner. We were trying to figure out who would put that stuff in our lockers. And you know, I think it was Vanessa! She all but admitted it out there in the hall. Why would she do such a terrible thing? And where would she get some of Joe's stuff?"

Karen sat down beside her and sighed. She looked out at the center of the gym, avoiding Bethany's eyes. "I've been taking crap all week. It's bad enough at home with my parents, and then I have to come here and listen to it."

"You mean your parents still haven't let up? Even after Angela talked to them?"

Karen slumped, resting her elbows on her knees. "Naw. They're like that. They get something in their heads, and that's it. You could bring out the Constitution of the United States and the Bible to prove them wrong, and it still wouldn't make any difference. I'm sorry about your jobs, but she isn't going to allow you to come back."

Karen shifted uneasily. "My parents are even talking about selling the diner and the drive-in and moving further out into the country. I can't stomach that. This is bad enough, but to be on top of a mountain somewhere . . . that would be my worst nightmare."

"Oh, Karen!" Bethany felt the anguish in her friend's eyes. "I don't know what to say!" Although Bethany admitted to herself that she liked Karen least of the Witches' Night Out members, this just wasn't fair.

Karen bowed her head, and even her ponytail seemed to droop. "What can you say? Nothing. I'll lose everything. My position on the cheerleading squad, Nick, all my friends. The only things that keep me going," She raised her head, looking straight at Bethany. "You don't know how bad it is at home, Bethany. Even before this happened. And now this is just one long descent into horror. I wish I'd never gotten into this Wicca stuff. It's royally screwed up my life!"

"Wicca isn't the reason this is happening, Karen," said Bethany softly. "It's called ignorance."

Karen looked away. "No, Bethany, it's because of Wicca. If I hadn't gotten into this in the first place, everything would be okay. It never occurred to me that my whole life could implode. I should *never* have gotten into magick. And you know, I've been thinking about it. There isn't any such thing. We were just a bunch of kids getting together because we were bored. The whole thing's a joke. Coincidence, you know?"

Bethany heard several kids entering the gym, their voices bouncing against the wooden bleachers, but she didn't bother to look up. It was probably Nam and Tillie, anyway. She'd told them to meet her here. "What are you trying to tell me, Karen?"

"That she doesn't want to be your friend anymore, Witch!"

Bethany looked up and into the colorless eyes of Vanessa the Viper, backed by several girls from the varsity cheerleading squad.

Vanessa tossed her long, honey-blonde hair. "Don't think you're so hot now, do you? You know," she whispered, eyes glittering, "they used to *burn* Witches!" Vanessa thrust out a lighter and flicked it under Bethany's hair.

Karen jumped up and slapped the lighter out of her hand. "Cut it out, Vanessa." She turned to Bethany. "You'd better go. And you can tell the others that I don't want to see them anymore, either."

Bethany's jaw dropped. She blinked. "Nick, too?"

Karen straightened her shoulders, her blue eyes turning a smoky-gray. "Nick agrees with me. He is my boyfriend, after all. He'll do whatever I say. Besides," she looked quickly at Vanessa, "he doesn't know anything about *your* little cult. If you don't get out of here now, I'll tell them about all the terrible stuff you claim you've done. Like hexing Mr. Kuhn. I even saw you put pig's blood on the football field so that our team would have a losing season! Take my word for it, you ladies are on your own." Her nail-bitten fingers dug around the collar of her shirt until they gripped the pentacle necklace. She jerked the chain, whipping the pentacle at Bethany's face. It missed, gliding across the high-gloss gym floor with a gentle, metallic sound.

Bethany watched the slow slide of the necklace as if her vision had geared down to slow motion. She could not believe the lies pouring out of Karen's mouth. Why would she say such terrible things? And why did she lie about misplacing her necklace, when clearly it had been around her neck the whole time? She wondered if Karen had helped Vanessa put that stuff in their lockers, which might explain why there wasn't anything in Nick's. But why would Karen do that? That would be more than stupid. Why implicate herself?

Bethany surveyed the hateful faces around her, including Karen's cool, stinging gaze. Each girl was dressed exactly the same, from the blue, gold, and white cheerleading uniform down to matching socks and white Nikes. She felt like clones surrounded her. A girl with fox-red hair, in her peripheral vision, face encased in a pound of makeup, produced another lighter. Several others followed her lead. Flick. Flick. Flick. Someone dodged at her eyes and she felt her lashes curl. She screamed, jerking her head away. She felt flames at her side, and stumbled toward a small opening in the ring of girls, the corner of her hockey letter-vest on fire, the double blue and gold CC flaming with a sickening odor.

Somewhere in the din she heard an adult yell, "Hey! What's going on over there?" Eyes swelling with hot tears, her chest heaving, Bethany ran from the gym, the smell of scorched hair in her nostrils, angry voices tidal-waving behind her. She tore off the vest, leaving the smoldering mess in the center of the hall.

Ramona did not look up from the five-gallon aluminum pot simmering on the stove. Hecate sat patiently at her feet, hoping for a tidbit. "You know, *mon cherie*," she said, the spoon in her hand sliding back and forth through the stew, "when someone treats me bad, I mix up a cup of sugar water. Then Ramona writes that person's name on a piece of paper." She tapped the spoon on the edge of the pot, bending close to the mixture. She sniffed two or three times. "Needs oregano. I put the paper and the sweet water in a plastic bag, and then I stuff the whole thing in the freezer. Calms things down a bit. Yes, that's what Ramona does. 'Course, if they burned my hair and ruined my favorite vest, I might add some vinegar to the sugar water, or maybe some red pepper."

The cat slithered around to the other side of Ramona, politely batting her leg with a dainty black paw to remind her that he was waiting patiently for a snack.

Dumbstruck, Bethany stood in the center of the kitchen. Ramona still hadn't turned around to face her. "How . . . how did you know?" whispered Bethany. Was this woman so incredibly psychic that she knew everything? "Does it work?"

Ramona added several spices to the stew, then threw Hecate a little piece of meat. The cat gobbled the prize. "As sure as I'm standing here," said Ramona.

Hecate hollered for more.

The housekeeper turned around, her hands on her hips. "Sometimes, the critters tell Ramona things . . . ," she said, looking down at Hecate, who gazed up at her with the closest look a cat could get to adoration without losing dignity.

"You mean you talk to animals?" exclaimed Bethany.

Ramona grinned, then shook her head. "Nah. Nam called, looking for you. She was worried. She is such a pretty girl, *no*? By the way, your father won't be home this weekend. He said for me to tell you that he has a double homicide, and that he was sorry. I'm to use the camera that takes moving pictures so he can see you in your new dress. The one you will buy to wear to the dance."

Bethany leaned up against the kitchen wall. "I'm not going."

Ramona glared at her. "Why not?"

Sighing, Bethany said, "First—I don't have a dress. I forgot to get one. Second—I don't have a date."

"So that stops a girl of the new millennium? You run in packs these days anyway, what does it matter?"

Bethany continued to stare at Ramona. She really wanted to say, "Because my date is dead. In the grave. Worms and bugs and fungus crawling all over his desiccating body." But instead she said, "I don't want to go."

"Ramona thinks you are being morose, *mon cherie*."

"Well, I guess it doesn't matter what good old Ramona thinks, does it?" spat Bethany. "You're just the housekeeper, not my mother!" She stomped out of the kitchen, flew up the stairs to her room, and slammed the door so hard the hinges rattled. It did not make her feel the least bit better.

Chapter 7

She told you to what?" asked Nam, rolling her shoulders and trying to shift her red backpack over her shoulders. The first frost last week painted the Cedar Crest High School campus in bright crimson, pumpkin, and gold. The girls plowed through piles of sweet-smelling leaves.

"To put the names of the people who are bothering me in sugar water and freeze the water," said Bethany.

Nam whistled. "So? Did you do it?"

They left the main sidewalk, rounding the corner onto the cobbled walk of the Cedar Crest library. Bethany exhaled slowly. "Well, yeah, I did it," she said sheepishly, eyeing Nam's color coordination flair for the day—purple, although those clunky shoes had a bit of silver on them. Bethany wondered if those silver patches would work like the night-reflecting tape that cyclists put on their clothing so they didn't get squashed on the highway.

Nam's green eyes looked at Bethany closely. "You know," she said. "I think Ramona is a real magickal person."

Bethany snorted. "What is your definition of a

real magickal person?"

"Oh, I don't know. Born into it, I guess."

"We weren't born into it, and we're magickal. Our spells work," replied Bethany with a defensive edge.

"No. I mean it," said Nam excitedly. "Maybe she's an old family tradition, or Hoodoo, or Voodoo, or Santeria? Kinda like Tillie."

"Tillie?"

"Well, sure! Tillie's grandma was a root doctor down south. I thought you knew that?"

Bethany shook her head. "She never told me."

"Funny," replied Nam. "Well, anyway, first," she stuck her index finger up and wiggled the purple nail, "Ramona wears white all the time. Second," the obliging second finger shot out, "she tells you about folk spells. Third," her ring finger joined the first two, "you can't hear her when she walks . . ."

"What?!"

Nam grinned. "Just wanted to make sure you were listening." Nam pushed her sleek black hair away from ivory cheeks. "And? So? You did the spell. And what?"

Bethany blushed and looked down at the brick walk littered with colorful leaves, embarrassed. "Nothing yet. I guess it's too soon to tell. I only did it this afternoon."

Nam pulled open the large glass and brass door of the library. "I still can't believe that Karen did that to you. Or to us! To be honest, I always thought I was the . . . well . . . weak one."

"Don't be so hard on yourself, Nam," responded Bethany, wishing for the hundredth time she hadn't included the girl in her latest Witches' Night Out scheme. She was just too nice to be mixed up in Joe's death. Bethany led the way to a secluded table in the corner. "I called Tillie and she said she'd meet us here." Her mind flitted uncomfortably over Tillie's lineage. Why had she told Nam, but not Bethany?

Nam set her backpack on the table and took off her purple coat. "What about Nick?"

"I don't know. He may be practicing with the team or he could be with Karen. I doubt we'll see him again, either. Like Karen said, Nick is her boyfriend. Why would he want to hang with us, especially now?"

Two freshman girls passed their table and giggled. Bethany could have sworn one of them muttered "Witch" under her breath. Bethany ignored them. "What are you doing your term paper on?" she asked, sitting down at the table and pawing through her backpack.

"ESP. Extrasensory perception," said Nam. Geez, she was even chewing purple gum. "How about you?"

"I don't know. I was thinking of doing a paper on the origins of Halloween."

Nam sat down beside her. "That sounds pretty good. Wish I'd thought of it first. Do you think Karen was telling the truth about Nick—that he won't want to be in our group anymore?"

"I don't know and I could care less," she said irritably, regretting the hurt she saw in Nam's eyes. "I'm sorry," she added quickly. "I didn't mean to take it out on you. But after her announcement about blood on the football field and our hexing Mr. Kuhn, we're lucky there isn't a lynch mob after us. I just can't believe her!"

"It's okay," said Nam quietly. "This is all so bizarre. Do you know Tillie and I got to the gym right after you left today, and Karen told us that you'd gotten sick and we should go and find you?"

"Figures."

"That's right, as if nothing terrible had happened. They're talking about suspending Vanessa and her friends for burning your vest, but I think the coach will get them off. What's a football game without cheerleaders?" Nam opened a notebook, twirling a pencil in her fingers. "And if she put that stuff in our lockers, well I hope she gets the same back in spades! What a sleaze!"

Anger swelled in Bethany's throat. "You know, she's warlocking," she said tightly.

"Who?"

"Karen. When a Witch turns traitor against their magickal friends, it's called warlocking. They used to put Witches to death for ratting on each other." Bethany's skin started to crawl. Something wasn't right. Maybe it was all this talk about Karen.

"So, it works!" said Tillie gleefully.

Nam and Bethany jumped, banging their chairs.

The librarian, who up to this time hadn't paid attention to them, shushed them with wag of her finger and a stern glare. Bethany stared at Tillie, now sitting beside them, with an open mouth. "One minute you weren't there, and then you appeared! How did you do that?"

Tillie giggled, earning them a biting look from the librarian. "I've been practicing glamoury. You know, changing the perception of yourself? I wanted to be invisible, and so I was!"

Nam nervously chewed the end of her eraser. "No way. Nobody can be invisible. It's not possible."

"You're right," said Tillie, "but you're not."

Nam bit through the purple eraser of her purple-barreled pencil. "Yuck!" she said, spitting the rubber out of her mouth. "I don't get it."

"You're not really invisible. People just think you are. The trick is to imagine a shield around yourself that people can't see through, but you can't make a noise and you can't look anyone directly in the eye. Then you've blown it. You guys were easy because you were so engrossed in your conversation."

"I don't know . . . ," said Nam, "but I'd like to learn that! I could have sworn you just materialized in that chair, like in a science fiction movie!"

The librarian stalked over to their table, her wild red frizzy hair pulled so tightly at her temples by multicolored plastic butterfly clips that her eyes were reduced to slits. "Ladies, if you can't keep it down, I'll have to ask you to leave." She turned on her combat-booted heel and walked briskly back to the front desk.

The girls broke into peals of laughter.

"What's so funny?" asked Nick, sliding into the seat beside Bethany.

The mood abruptly changed. "What are you doing here?" asked Bethany, feeling the edge in her own voice. Had he come to spy on them for Karen?

Nick played with the zipper on his football jacket. "I seem to miss all the good stuff," he said, not really looking at any of them. "I've heard a couple of different stories, but it doesn't matter." He swallowed hard. "Karen and I broke up." He laid a silver pentacle on the table, its beveled edges catching the light. No one said anything.

"We haven't been getting along for awhile, anyway," he said. "This whole mess just finished the relationship off. Here's her coven necklace. She's convinced you're going to curse her if she doesn't give it back." He threw the circular pendant on the library table. They all watched the pentacle design, surrounded by the eight phases of the moon, spin with a hollow, echoing sound. As if exhausted, it suddenly plunked, the pentacle winking in the library light.

"That's ridiculous!" snorted Tillie, pushing the necklace toward Nick. "Get rid of it. Anything circular continues to hold the energy of the person who wore it. We certainly don't want any of Karen's negative behavior to rub off on us! Bury it!"

Nam nodded, her green eyes wide and dark.

Bethany shook her head. "I'm so sorry, Nick. None of us ever meant for any of this to happen. But I talked to Karen this afternoon. She was so sincere about how much you mean to her . . ."

Nick's jaw hardened. "Don't sweat it. Karen certainly isn't suffering. She's going to the homecoming dance with Todd Lancaster."

Tillie pounded the table with her fist, earning a disapproving glance from the librarian. "That's terrible!" she said.

"I don't believe it," muttered Nam.

Bethany said nothing, understanding the grief her friend felt. If Joe had done that to her, she would've just died. Her stomach twisted. Bad use of terminology. She looked around the table. There was such a feeling of togetherness here. How could any one of them hurt Joe? She wished she had Tillie's knack for picking up other people's feelings—then she might know for sure. Then she could trust them. This was all so complicated!

One thing was factual. Now none of them had dates for the dance, and any hope of being asked, at this point, was nil. They were definitely the outcasts of the school, except Nick, and once he was seen with them, he would be, too. Bethany opened her mouth to say something about that, but then snapped it shut. Nick wasn't stupid. He could make his own choices.

Instead, she said, "Since none of us are going to the dance, why don't we meet at the bowling alley tomorrow night? I mean, it's something to do."

Tillie nodded. "Sounds like a good idea."

Nam sucked on her lower lip. "You know, I don't want to stop Witches' Night Out. It's too much fun. I really wanted to get together this past Thursday, but I didn't want to push my parents too far."

Tillie nodded in agreement. "Yeah, my dad's congregation told him they are looking for a replacement. I didn't want to make him feel bad."

Nick nodded. "Even though Marissa probably wouldn't have been awake, I didn't want to risk it."

Guilt hit Bethany square in the face. These people were being so nice, wanting to stick together no matter what. How could she have thought that any one of them had been involved in Joe's death? But part of her said, *Don't let your guard down. Don't do it. Not yet.*

"What is going on with your sister, Nick?" asked Tillie.

Nick cracked his knuckles, not looking at any of them. "Right now, she has twenty-four-hour care from a visiting nurse, but if she doesn't snap out of it soon, the doctors are talking about committing her. There's some new ones looking at her now. I'd hate to see them decide to put her away. Before all this mess, she was unbelievably intelligent. A little crazy, maybe, but nice. This new doctor thinks that her condition is a result of drug use while she was in high school, and I think he might be right. She always seemed stoned, but my parents were so busy with their careers, they didn't notice. The doctor is asking me a lot of questions and I've called some of her old friends. She was into shit she shouldn't have been."

Bethany took a shower and put on her favorite nightgown. The clock downstairs chimed, the sound almost lost to her ears as it filtered through her bedroom door. Hecate was kneading her pillow, waiting impatiently for her to go to bed.

She picked up Joe's photo on her dresser and stared at those liquid brown eyes, that sexy grin, the lock of dark hair playing across his forehead. Gone. Taken out by a predator. She was sure of it.

Bethany's father talked about predators all the time. It was, after all, a part of his job, but she'd seen that voracious look in her own father's eyes when he was after a criminal. When he thought he'd solved a case. She looked at her own dark eyes in the mirror. Was she predator or prey? Or could a person be both? Wasn't her own father a predator of criminals but the prey of a beautiful, ambitious woman? Bethany carefully set Joe's photo back in its place.

She sat on the edge of the bed, rubbing Hecate's back. His loud purr echoed in the room. What did she remember about Joe's last day? A shiver tickled her arms and clutched at her back. For weeks her mind danced, always doing an intricate jig away from the facts, away from the pain. She knew it was time she faced those hurtful memories.

As she drifted into sleep, the howling of a dog from somewhere outside refused to let her slip into total dream bliss.

She slept restlessly on the edge.

Chapter 8

"What are you doing?" asked Bethany.

"Ah! *Mon cherie!* Ramona thinks that it is high time we make sure that no bad people get inside the house." She spread an assortment of dead green plant bits along the entrance to the front door. The strong aroma of cinnamon, oranges, and something else, something musky, assaulted Bethany's nose. Hecate sat on the staircase, supervising the whole affair. Bethany put her hands behind her back, contemplating the housekeeper. If this wasn't magick, she didn't know what was. "And I suppose most normal housekeepers do this kind of thing in Louisiana?"

Ramona shrugged. "Some do. Some don't," she said, allowing the herb mixture to filter through her brown fingers onto the floor, muttering something in French under her breath.

"If this keeps Angela out, I'm all for it."

"Hmmm," answered Ramona.

Hecate yawned.

Bethany considered what she should say next. "Um, Ramona? I . . . I just wanted to apologize for my behavior yesterday. I'm sorry for being so mean.

You know, when I screamed at you and ran up the stairs?"

The housekeeper threw more of the herbal mixture on the floor. Finally, she turned and faced Bethany. "Ramona says that's okay. You were upset. Just don't let it happen again."

Couldn't this woman ever talk properly? Bethany ached to remind the housekeeper that the personage of Ramona and the housekeeper were one in the same, but she thought better of it as she'd just apologized for being such an idiot. Hecate raised a small black paw, licking daintily.

Ramona eyed Bethany. "Going somewhere?"

Bethany plastered her best smile across her face, shifting the weight of her purple bowling bag. "Yes," she said, "since we're not going to the dance, we decided to go bowling."

Ramona looked at her watch. "It is only three. Your bowling starts early."

"Oh no! I'm going over to Tillie's house. We're going to eat and then go together."

"Dinner?" questioned Ramona.

"At Tillie's house," Bethany answered.

"Be back before midnight."

She left Ramona clucking her tongue and talking to the cat in French as she hurried down the walk to her car.

It was a very weird autumn. Today, the sun shone brightly, the temperatures hitting a record eighty-two degrees. Bethany could feel herself sweating profusely under her sweatshirt. The heavy material felt like it weighed a ton. Tillie lived in a quaint, white frame house with green shutters close to her father's church. Bethany always admired the yard, with its magickal double willows and multitude of flowers. Today was no exception. Tillie's mother was tending buckets and baskets of fall mums. She smiled as Bethany marched up the walk.

"She's up in her room," said Mrs. Alexander, wiping the sweat off her brow with the back of her dirt-smudged garden glove. "I'm glad you girls are going out. Put this awful mess behind you. Everything always looks so much brighter when there is a little bit of fun. I wish you kids would have gone to the dance, though. All those pretty dresses, music and smiles . . ." her voice drifted as she stared into space, probably remembering dances past.

Bethany smiled. She wished she had parents like Tillie's. Then again, maybe not. The dance could be the worst place for them right now. Anything might happen there, given Karen's habit of inciting riots. Bethany's school was an unusual mix—part townies, part kids from local farms, and part offspring of the professionals who fled the city in hopes of hiding their children from the violence of the streets. This unusual cultural mix did not mesh easily, or well. They all seemed to be on the edge. Waiting to make something happen. Good or bad, it didn't matter. That was why Bethany had started Witches'

Night Out in the first place. She wanted to make a positive place for like-minded kids to go.

Bethany looked at the front of the house. Tillie was considered a townie because she lived within the borough limits, though she didn't usually hang with the other townies, nor did she particularly care for the farm kids. Which either left outcasts like Bethany and Karen, who didn't fit anywhere, or the progeny of the rich—Nam and Nick. Of course, if Nick's sister kept running up the medical bills, Bethany wasn't sure how long they'd be able to hold on to their nice house on the hill, and all the other play toys of the well-to-do. She grimaced.

Not her problem.

Tillie was waiting for Bethany at the front door, a big grin on her face. "Hey! Mom's making lasagna for dinner and we'll toss the salad around five. That okay with you?"

Bethany's stomach rumbled at the thought, her mouth automatically salivating. Tillie's mom made the best lasagna. "What should we do until then?" asked Bethany.

"I think we need a real look-see at what's going on," said Tillie, bounding up the stairs to her third-floor room, Bethany at her heels. "I was going to suggest it right after Joe's death, but . . . well, I was afraid to call you."

Guilt again pounded at Bethany's temples.

Tillie opened the door to her room, only to find her eleven-year-old brother going through her CD collection. "Hey, Jake! Get out of here. MOM!"

Jake grinned, grabbed two CDs, and fled down the stairs.

"Brothers!" moaned Tillie.

"I don't know," replied Bethany. "I think it would be neat to have a brother or sister."

"Not if you really had one," said Tillie. "Trust me. I think we should do a reading before we go out tonight. With Karen saying all that stuff, well . . . someone might get zealous. Like I said, I would have called you before, but . . . I'm sorry I wasn't there for you."

Bethany cringed internally.

"So," said Tillie, smiling. "I'd like to make it up to you." She pulled a beautifully carved box out of her dresser drawer.

Bethany felt a nervous twinge. Of her six comrades, only Tillie managed to make any sense out of the Tarot, and she was good. Bethany didn't know if she felt comfortable with Tillie nosing into her past, but her desire to find the truth outweighed the risk.

Tillie fanned the cards. "Forewarned is forearmed. What question should we ask?"

Bethany threw her purse on the spread of Tillie's yellow canopy bed and began picking up the CDs that Jake left on the floor. "I'm not sure. Should we ask about our evening, or should we ask about Joe?" She was secretly hoping Tillie would pick the future, rather than delve into the past, but if she acted that way, Tillie would be suspicious.

Tillie sat on the bed. "Let's do both. You first. We'll do a three-card spread for you," she said. "Pick three cards out of the pack and put them on the bedspread."

Bethany did as instructed. She didn't like the look of those three cards. Not at all.

"Interesting," said Tillie.

Bethany felt like a bug under a microscope. She tucked her heavy hair behind her ears. "So, what do they say?"

Tillie pointed at the first card. "Past. Ten of Swords. You think it can't get any worse than it already is."

Bethany didn't like the look of that card. It showed a man with swords sticking out of his back and blood all over the place. Gruesome.

Tillie's finger moved to the second card. "The Present. Eight of Swords. Bound by your own fears or the words of others."

Bethany liked that card even less. It showed a woman bound by a rope, surrounded by swords. "Geez, Tillie, these are gross."

Tillie's mouth twitched. "Not all the cards in the deck have blood and swords on them. Most of them are pretty nice, actually. The last card is The Tower. Oh, honey, you'd better be careful! Basically this one means that your world is going to turn upside down, and you may not like it very much. However, in the end, you'll probably be better for it."

"Oh, how truly morbid and bleak," moaned

Bethany, wishing she hadn't let Tillie do this reading. "Throw down some more. What else does it say?"

Tillie held out the pack. "Pick two more."

Bethany took awhile to choose the cards. She wanted good ones. Happy ones. She handed her selection to Tillie, who turned the cards over one at a time.

"Justice!" she said, eyes shining. "That means that the right thing will definitely happen."

"But the woman on the card is blindfolded," said Bethany. "What does that mean?"

"That we often have to look within to find the truth. The truth isn't always apparent."

"I see. And the next one?" asked Bethany, holding her breath.

"Judgement," said Tillie.

This card depicted people rising from their coffins to the tune of an angel's horn.

"Bleck!" said Bethany.

"It's okay. It means things coming back to haunt you. Sometimes good. Sometimes bad. It's sort of a conclusion card, though it isn't necessarily the final chapter in the story. With it falling beside Justice, I would say that the truth will bring issues and put them right in front of your face. You'll have to deal."

"Wonderful," said Bethany, running her fingers over the smooth card. "Just what I need. Tillie, why didn't you ever tell me that your grandmother was a root doctor?"

Tillie fingered the cards absently. "Sorry. I thought you knew. Why? Does it make some sort of difference?"

Bethany looked at Tillie carefully, scanning her facial expression for deceit. She detected nothing. "I. I just wish you'd have told me, is all," she said, realizing how lame her response sounded.

Tillie shuffled the deck again. "It's no big deal. My father refuses to talk about it, but now and then, Mom will come out with a bit of folklore or a quaint superstition. They won't really tell me much more."

Bethany stared at her friend. "So, it's in your blood."

"What is?"

"The magick. You feel the magick, don't you? How it courses through your body?"

Tillie looked confused. "Doesn't it work like that for everybody?"

"I don't think so," replied Bethany.

"Well, you don't have any magick in your family and you feel the same way I do, don't you?" asked Tillie.

Bethany bit her bottom lip. "Yeah. Sure."

Tillie smiled. "Now, let's look at what happened to Joe."

Chapter 9

Tillie continued to shuffle the cards, staring into space, then began to lay them out in a cross pattern with extra cards running up the side.

"What did you get?" asked Bethany, a cold sensation gripping her intestines. She could turn back now. She could tell Tillie to forget it.

Tillie frowned. "I'm not sure. I just said, tell me about Joe's last week, and thought about what little we do know, so I'm not sure if I influenced the cards or not." She pointed to the card in the center of the cross. "That's The Fool, meaning, I think, that he was ready to do something new. Step off into a different direction. See how the little man in the picture is sort of on a hike, whistling while he walks? But he's headed for a cliff, so it could mean that Joe's idea wasn't such a hot idea, and he should have thought carefully before moving ahead. Does this make any sense to you?"

Bethany shifted uncomfortably.

Tillie moved to the second card, lying horizontally across the first. "This is what crossed him, the Five of Swords. Fights, arguments, possibly losing friends. Someone didn't approve of what he wanted to do, or maybe more than a single someone." She looked up at Bethany. "Any of this clicking for you?"

Bethany did not reply. Should she trust Tillie?

Tillie laid a third card on top of the second. "This card shows what or who put the block there in the first place. It's the High Priestess. She's sometimes a woman, sometimes a secret." Tillie didn't look up, but laid another card next to the High Priestess. "The Five of Pentacles. Possible affair. Feeling out in the cold." She drew another card from the pack. "The Page of Cups. Can be a boy or girl. Usually dreamy. Talented. Sometimes a message of love."

Tillie sat back and surveyed the cards. "Looks to me like you and Joe had a fight about another girl."

Bethany shuddered. Part of the secret out. What should she do?

"If you don't want to tell me about it, you don't have to," said Tillie slowly, her hands moving to gather up the remaining cards. "I can understand why you're hesitating to tell me anything. I haven't been all that great of a friend."

Bethany's eyes concentrated on Tillie's slender, brown hands. "No. No, that's okay." She decided to take the risk, so before she could change her mind, she plunged on. "Yes, we had a fight. Part of it was about another girl. Vanessa the Viper."

Tillie's ebony eyes rounded. "The Vanessa Peters who tried to burn your hair? The one you think put that stuff in our lockers?"

"There is only one Vanessa in our school, Tillie,"

said Bethany, irritation sliding up and down her arms like a rusty saw. "She'd been coming on to Joe. He thought it was a joke. Told me I was stupid for doubting how much he loved me. But he was proud, you know. Like . . . turned on because she was running after him like a crazy fool. I caught her at his house a few times. Joe swore they were just hanging out, but . . . she had that sultry, rumpled look. You know? I think now that he was messing with her. How else could she have gotten his ritual dagger?"

"Karen could have given it to her."

"That's possible, but how could Karen have gotten it? At the time, it really bothered me, but . . ."

Tillie leaned forward. "Yes?"

"But the real argument was about the picture."

"What picture?"

"The one on my bedroom dresser."

Tillie sat back. "Oh. So what about it?"

Bethany got up from the bed and walked around the room, hugging herself. "It was Marissa's idea."

"Nick's sister?" Tillie couldn't have looked more astonished if she'd seen a real live alien. "What does *she* have to do with this?"

Bethany sat back down on the bed. "Everything and nothing. It was her idea to have that freelance photographer come in from the *New York Times*. Something about an article on New York state up-and-coming teens. Joe wanted to get into a fancy college and he was working toward a scholarship. Some guy at the *Times* owed Marissa a favor. He's the one that got hold of the photographer. Marissa thought that if they added Joe to their list, it would help him."

Tillie looked confused. "Why would she care what happened to Joe?"

Miserable, Bethany continued pacing. "I don't know. Nick and Joe were best friends. They did everything together. All the guy stuff. Even so, I thought Marissa's attention was so strange. She seemed to have some sort of fascination or something. Why didn't she get her friend to do something on Nick? I mean, he's smart. Class president. In several sports. Lots of money. Perfect candidate for that kind of attention."

"You don't think . . ."

"Joe swore that she only wanted to help him because he was interested in journalism. And," she slapped her open palms on her thighs, "I believed him. She's too old for him, anyway," she said quickly.

"So why would that make you mad?"

Bethany threw her arms up in the air. "I don't know! I just had a bad feeling about the whole thing. None of it made sense. I was angry about Vanessa. It really bothered me that Marissa was constantly calling about that stupid article. I realized that when Joe went to college next year, I'd still be stuck in high school. There would be lots of girls like Vanessa—older girls—going after him. I was jealous. It was horrid. We had such an awful fight!" Unshed tears built pressure on her eyes, making them ache. Bethany pressed her fingers on her eyelids, willing herself to control her wild emotions.

"And that's it?" asked Tillie.

"No," Bethany muttered, taking a deep breath and forcing herself to act calmly. "Something else. Something weird. Joe got to be buds with this photographer guy, a Paul Neri. He even spent a few weekends with him in the city. Marissa found out about it and really chewed Joe out."

"This is before your big fight, right?"

Bethany nodded. "Yeah," she said, pacing the floor and hugging herself. "I mean, why would Marissa care what Joe did?"

"Do you think he was getting involved in something dangerous?"

Bethany stopped, turning around slowly. "I don't know. He wasn't into drugs, or alcohol, or kinky stuff. Just a plain old local football hero. He told Marissa to buzz off. Like I said, it was too weird. Joe told me that Marissa belonged in the loony bin. Did you know that she went through her house and burned all the pictures of her parents?"

Tillie shook her head. "Nick never said anything that I know of."

"Well, she did, and she sold all the engraved silver stuff from their twenty-fifth wedding anniversary, and not because she needed the money either. They had tons."

Tillie had her hands in a prayerful position, covering her mouth. "What does the photographer guy have to do with all of this?" she asked.

Bethany flapped her hands in the air. "Maybe nothing. Maybe everything. I just don't know. When no one would believe me about Joe's accident, well, I just sort of stewed over it for the last two months. I know, deep in my heart, that something isn't right. When Marissa burst into my house I just couldn't believe it!"

"Did Joe ever give you any idea? Anything at all?"

Bethany's voice quivered. "He told me he loved me more than anything in the world. That he'd never do anything to hurt me and that he was preparing for our future. He told me that he had something big. So big and so unreal that none of us in Cedar Crest would ever believe it. He said he was sorry for making me feel bad. And then he handed me that stupid framed picture, told me to think of him, and drove off. He was to meet us for Witches' Night Out later and, well . . . you know the rest. I never saw him again."

"That is so strange," said Tillie, looking down at the cards. She pointed to the past position. "Eight of Wands. A trip. I guess that was to the city. Ahead of him, The Lovers card. This could have been his relationship with you, but it also stands for big contracts and negotiations, especially with the Two of Wands and Three of Pentacles beside it. Someone offered him a deal."

"But what about his college?" asked Bethany.

"I don't know," said Tillie. "I'm not sure." She looked at the remaining cards. "What crowns him— The Devil. He was fooling himself. What he rests on—The Star, his hopes and dreams for the future. Not a bad card, though The Devil always means trouble. With The Emperor beside it—hmmm, possible incarceration."

"I can't believe that," said Bethany. "He was so . . . well . . . he had such a Boy Scout mentality."

Tillie shrugged. "Even the best people occasionally have very nasty secrets." She waved her hands over the remainder of the cards. "I haven't put the outcome cards out yet, because I thought we should read everything else first. This is interesting . . . under the Karma position—things that the person should have learned? He's got the Seven of Cups, meaning all that glitters isn't gold, followed by the Seven of Swords and The Moon. Definite deception by people he knows."

Bethany fidgeted with her thick hair, curling a piece at her temple around her finger. Tillie looked at her strangely. "You thought that we, the circle members, might have something to do with his death, didn't you? That's why you called us all back together."

Bethany swallowed, the saliva clumped in her throat, her eyes running from her friend's hard gaze.

Tillie was silent. They could hear her brother downstairs, arguing with his mother about getting washed up for supper. Somewhere outside the window a lawn mower roared to life.

Finally, Tillie said, "Why would you think that?"

"Because I'm sure it was someone who knew

him. And you all spent the most time with him."

"But . . . killers? You thought we were *killers*? That's against all of the Wiccan Principles of Belief! How could you *think* that?"

Bethany felt sick to her stomach. She slumped to the floor, hot tears flowing from her aching eyes. "I don't know. I just don't *know!* I had so much hatred inside. So much!" She leaned over, burying her face in her hands.

Tillie got up and walked over, gently holding Bethany. "It's okay. I'm so sorry. It just never dawned on me how much pain you must have been in. To suspect your best friends. How scary."

"Who *killed* him?" sobbed Bethany.

"So far," said Tillie, "there isn't a face card here that indicates that."

Bethany sighed. Hiccuped. "Figures."

Tillie resumed her place on the bed, while Bethany scrubbed the tears from her eyes with the back of her hand. Tillie looked at the last few cards. "Under other's impressions, there isn't much here. A mixed bag, of sorts. Some cups, some wands, no swords or pentacles, no major arcana. It appears the closest people to him thought he had a great future."

"That's odd," said Bethany. "You'd think that there would be swords there, representing the person that killed him."

"Not if it was a legitimate accident," said Tillie. "Or, it could mean that circumstances dictated his death more so than an individual person, or that the person who killed him hadn't intended to, or didn't know him very well. I'm going to skip his hopes and dreams, if you don't mind."

Bethany nodded, a weak sniffle escaping from her lips.

"Now, for the outcome." She laid down four cards and whistled. "The Chariot reversed, the Ten of Swords, the Eight of Swords, and the Ace of Swords." She sighed. "Basically, this spells D-E-A-T-H."

"Why not the Death card?" asked Bethany, shivering.

"Because the Death card means radical change, not physical death. I didn't expect it to be here, and would have been really surprised if it was. The Chariot reversed, I think, stands for the car accident, especially with the swords beside it, indicating that Fate was dealing her final blow . . . oh, sorry," she said, looking up at Bethany's tight face. "I sort of got carried away there."

"But no answer to who killed him?"

"None. Like I said, these cards do not rule out an accident."

"Lay down another card."

"I don't see the point," Tillie said, hesitating. "I mean, he *is* dead. The story's over."

Bethany shook her head. "But the story isn't over, don't you see? It won't be over until we know who killed him."

"Look, Bethany, maybe we should just quit."

"No! Throw down another card, please!"

Tillie threw down another card. "The Tower." She placed one more card on the bright yellow bed-spread. "Justice," she whispered.

"One more," urged Bethany.

Tillie wavered, then laid down a third card. Judgement. "This is too weird," she breathed. "They're the same three cards in your reading."

"What's that supposed to mean?"

Tillie slapped her hands on her knees. "Basically, your future is linked to his past," she hesitated. "You'll discover the truth, but you may not like it." Tillie's dark eyes wavered on Bethany, "Listen. Did you . . . Did you say anything about Marissa or the photographer to Joe's parents . . . or to your dad?"

"I tried to, but no one would listen to me. It's like, if there was even the hint of anything bad, they didn't want to know."

Tillie picked up the cards and put them back in the small wooden box. "Did you talk to Marissa?"

"Every time I phoned her, she hung up on me. I even went over to their house once. She wouldn't answer the door."

Tillie started changing into jeans and a soft, forest green shirt. "Did you ask Nick?" came the muffled question as she slipped the shirt over her head, the satin material rippling into place.

"I tried to ask him at the funeral, but he gave me the cold shoulder. I was surprised when he agreed to come to Witches' Night Out the first week of school. He told me when I called him that he was sorry he acted like such a jerk. He said it was his way of grieving."

Tillie zipped up her jeans. "So, did you ask him then?"

"Nah. What was I going to say? Everyone in town knows Marissa is unbalanced. She got fired from the newspaper right after Joe's death. Then she accosted a grocery store clerk and told the cops that the clerk was a part of some big conspiracy to kill her. I'm really surprised they didn't put her away then, but her doctors said she was hallucinating because they gave her the wrong psychotropic drugs."

"How do you know all this?" asked Tillie, straightening her shirt.

"My dad's a cop. Remember? People tell him lots of things. I don't know why they do it, other than they want to be friendly with the law so if something happens, they'll have a friend in the system. They feed him all sorts of gossip about other people, thinking my dad won't pay too much attention to them. It's strange."

Tillie pulled on a pair of orange sneakers.

Bethany laughed and made a cross with her fingers. "Yuck!"

"Hey, I like 'em," said Tillie, smiling sheepishly, but her expression turned serious. "So, you've been inadvertently using your father for information? Isn't that . . . well . . . dishonest?"

Bethany cocked an eyebrow. "I've been watching. And waiting. Since when is that dishonest?"

Chapter 10

The warm weather of the afternoon turned spiteful, Indian summer retreating from the heavy skirts of Mother Winter. Bethany shivered, cranking up the heat in the car. They both screamed when someone knocked on the steamed windows.

"Hey, what are you guys doing in there?" came Nick's muffled voice.

Tillie opened the car door and slid out, adjusting her fringed leather jacket. "Retro," Tillie said as she threw the heavy coat on before they left the house. Now, the fringes whipped against the coat as a shuddering, cold blast of air swirled around the parking lot.

Bethany turned off the engine and followed, extracting both their bowling bags from the trunk. The chilly wind caught her hair, slapping stinging ends in her eyes. She blinked rapidly, catching her tears with a brush of numb fingers. "I wish this weather would make up its mind," she muttered, handing Tillie her bowling bag. A dented plastic cup did a precarious jig across the parking lot of Bindle Bowl. Closing the lid of the trunk, she asked, "What time is it?"

Laughter spilled from the open doors of the squat brick building like bits of sharp glass raining against a tin roof. Nick checked his watch. "Ten after seven. I wonder where Nam is?"

The three of them stood beside the Camaro, shivering, looking up at the threatening sky and listening to the click of the engine as it quickly cooled.

"Why don't we go in and get a lane? She can find us by asking at the desk," said Tillie.

Bindle Bowl seemed to crawl with just about every breathing human from the tricounty area. Bethany and her friends squirmed through the crowd in the doorway, past the glass-enclosed bar where billows of cigarette smoke puffed like a steam engine whenever the door opened or closed. The snack counter to their right belched sizzling French fries and gallons of counter-sticky soda.

"Looks like everyone had the same idea," Bethany shouted over the din of human chatter rivaling the background sonata of strikes, spares, and gutter balls laced with pounding country music. Tillie shook her head, her raised eyebrows indicating this was not a good idea. Bethany raised her hands, then dropped them to her sides. "It's either this, or we go home and stew there," she said.

Tillie headed for the lane reservation counter and returned several minutes later. "There's a forty-five minute wait for a lane," grumped Tillie. "Let's get a table at the snack bar and keep our eyes open for Nam."

Nick shouldered through the crowd near the counter and found them an empty but littered table. It took the waitress fifteen minutes to get to them, clean the table, and take their order.

While they waited, Bethany watched several kids in party outfits filter through the brightly colored chaos of bowling uniforms and blue jeans. As several girls flounced by the table, Bethany stopped one girl dressed in a red, slinky dress and sparkling hose. "Why aren't you at the dance?"

"Some stupid cheerleaders tried to burn that Witch girl yesterday in the gym. The new principal was so angry he waited until we all got there, gave us a speech, and cancelled the dance. I hope that girl really does go up in flames!" she said, cocking her head defiantly. "I spent two hundred dollars on this dress! Just wait until I get my hands on those stupid cheerleaders!" The girl jerked her hand back and continued to elbow her way through the crowd.

"Wow," said Tillie. "No way!"

Nick shook his head. "Obviously she has no idea who you are."

"Obviously," said Bethany as their pizza arrived.

"I wonder where Nam is?" asked Tillie, twirling the steaming cheese of the deep-dish pizza around her finger before she popped it in her mouth.

Bethany gave Tillie a disgusted look. "You just had two plates of lasagna not less than an hour ago. How can you be hungry? And then stay so thin! It's positively sinful."

Tillie slurped a fat mushroom smothered in sauce. "I just think myself thin."

"Oh, *please!*" said Nick, picking at the crust on his pizza.

A chorus of shouts filtered around them from the wax-slick lanes. Tillie picked up another piece of pizza.

Bethany's gaze drifted past the table beside them filled with three middle-aged women sipping sodas and telling bawdy jokes. They laughed loudly, one of them spilled her soda, but the shock of what she saw beyond them made her jaw drop. Karen hanging all over Todd Lancaster. Bethany moved closer to Nick, trying to block his view, but she was too late. The muscles at his temples drew back, and a strange empty look entered his eyes.

Karen saw them, laughed loudly, and planted a kiss on Todd's heavy lips. She swiveled a hip encased in an electric blue mini skirt and ran her fingers softly down her new love's face. Nick gripped the edge of the table, rocking the flimsy metal legs.

Tillie muttered, "Oh, my stars!" as she looked past Bethany's shocked expression.

Out of her peripheral vision, Bethany sensed more than saw someone approaching their table from the opposite side. She looked up in surprise as a short man, dressed in chinos and a black bomber jacket, tapped Bethany on the shoulder. "Mind if I sit down?" he asked, flipping a metal chair around and straddling it.

"Excuse me?" said Bethany, checking out the short dark hair and clean shaven cheeks. His eyes reminded her of the prehistoric science exhibit at the museum, the one with large clumps of amber encasing big, black, dead bugs. He adjusted the oversized jacket, as if he was too large for it. Bethany was not impressed.

"I understand you're Bethany Salem," he said, the syllables flowing crisply, his jacket creaking as he leaned forward to balance his chin on the red chair back. Bethany noticed an expensive camera slung over his shoulder.

Nick's eyelids plunged to slits. "Who wants to know?"

The stranger relaxed, leaning on the back of the chair. "My name is Paul Neri. Perhaps you've heard of me? I was a friend of Joe's. I'm a freelance photo-journalist based out of New York City. Joe was a real con man. He would have either become a very rich man or landed in prison in his old age. I've had a lot of time on my hands, business is slow, so I got to thinking." He rolled his shoulders. "And I figure that his death wasn't an accident." He scratched his nose. "I smell a story. A big one. High school superstar dies in a freak car accident. Then, a friend of mine in town calls me and lets me know about you." He pointed at Bethany. "Joe's girlfriend and her pals get kicked out of school for belonging to some sort of cult, and that's only for starters . . ." He reached over and tore off a small section of pizza and popped it in his mouth, chewing loudly.

Bethany's pulse raced. She didn't like the flat look in this man's odd, golden eyes.

"Should I add," he said, licking a stubby finger, "that a fancy lawyer blows in and decimates the principal and half the school board. A dance for over 1,500 students is canceled because a little cheerleader got overzealous with a lighter and tries to put said girlfriend and best athlete on the hockey team to a test of fire. Then, lo and behold, I hear on my scanner that one of said pals is a victim of a car accident."

Nick leaned forward. "What are you talking about? What accident?"

Paul Neri aimed his blunt fingers at a squashed straw paper on the table and flicked it onto the floor. "I think it's real unusual that such good friends would be sitting in a bowling alley, eating pizza, while their supposed best friend goes under the knife."

Bethany could feel the group mind coalesce. Confusion. Anger. Rage. Fear. Protection. Oh, they were missing Nam and Karen, but numbers didn't necessarily mean anything. Except they really weren't missing Karen physically. She was here. Bethany scanned the crowd, her eyes capturing Karen's. Karen dropped her hands from her new boyfriend, a moment of what—recognition?—then her face turned to a visage of Roman stone. She looked at Bethany, then at Paul Neri. The mental wall around them grew stronger. Perhaps Karen hadn't left them, after all. What did this yahoo journalist want, anyway? What accident? What *was* he talking about?

Paul Neri stood up, straightening his leather jacket. "No one's pointed any fingers at you three, yet. And I'm wondering about that little cheerleader over there. See, Joe talked about all of you. I sort of got sick of hearing it, but then . . . lookie here. I might just get a good story after all. Could have been the four of you killed him. You know, a cult thing. Maybe the little cheerleader knew what you did, so she's keeping her distance. I, however, am a *very* patient man. When this story breaks, I'm going to be all over you and your little pals," he sneered.

He placed his two doughy hands on the table and leaned forward, lowering his voice to a whisper. "Because I think you murdered Joe. Nam Chu got nervous, so you tried to get rid of her. Too bad you didn't succeed, because as soon as she wakes up, she'll point that adolescent hysteria at you."

Something clutched at Bethany's heart. Squeezing. Squeezing. Squeezing. "What about Nam?" asked Bethany, her voice little more than a rasp of air. "What do you mean? What's happened to Nam?"

Tillie rose from her chair, her face a mask of terror.

Neri waved his thick hand in the air. "I just wanted you to know that I'm on to you. I think I'll go talk to that little blonde over there. I'm sure she can help unravel this mystery."

Bethany could feel the scream building at the bottom of her throat, threatening to explode even if she took so much as a teeny tiny breath.

Nick jumped to his feet, grabbing Paul's arm. "You so much as touch her and I'll flatten you."

Paul violently shrugged off Nick's grip. "Is that a statement for the record?"

"Take it however you want," growled Nick.

"What happened to Nam?" asked Tillie, the edge on her voice so sharp the women at the next table grew silent.

Paul Neri smiled, a touch of wolf playing on his lips. "You mean you really don't know? Nice acting, kids. I don't remember any of you being involved in the drama club, but you should be. Well. I'll play along. Your little Chinese friend got smashed to smithereens on Orr Bank Road less than an hour ago. Flew her to Mercy Hospital, she was in such bad shape."

Bethany's mind could not cope. She sat there, stunned, the colors and sounds of Bindle Bowl flashing around her like the view from the worst roller coaster ride in history. First Joe, now Nam? It just wasn't possible!

Paul Neri was still talking. "Good stories mean big money. Besides, that Joe kid owed me."

Bethany found her voice as she rose from the table. "I think you're lying! How did Joe owe you?"

"Bunch of pictures I took for him. Extra ones. He could have at least paid me before he met the big football hero in the sky, if you know what I mean."

Bethany stepped forward, anger replacing frustration. She grabbed Neri by the front of his bomber jacket. People at the other tables were looking at them, but she didn't care. "You are a vile man!" she exclaimed, jerking the front of his jacket.

Paul knocked her arms away. "Keep your hands to yourself, trailer trash," he said angrily. "Joe and I, we had a business deal."

Tillie stood beside Bethany. "Harassing a minor can lead to prison time, chum. Back off."

Paul shrugged, fingers playing with the camera. "Do you want to confess? Maybe this place is too open." He stepped closer to Bethany. "Want to come talk to me privately? Tell Paulie all about it? How you arranged for your friend to die? How you ran the pretty Chinese girl off the road? Tried to kill her?" He drifted his fingers lightly under her chin. "I think you're a very evil little girl," he whispered.

"No!" wailed Bethany.

Neri leaned over and kissed her.

Bethany turned her head, the slimy kiss blazing across her cheek. "If you know so much, why haven't you gone to the cops?" she asked, resisting the urge to spew the contents of her stomach all over this horrid man.

"Proof, baby," he said softly. "Proof." He backed up and snapped a picture in her face, the flash of the camera temporarily blinding her.

Nick sprung forward but Paul was too quick for

him, sidestepping deftly and pushing Nick into a group of metal chairs. Nick went down hard, his temple covered in blood. Karen's thin scream floated through the air. Bethany was so angry that for a moment, her rational mind completely left her. Rage curled her fingers. "The strength of the Dark Mother within me!" she screamed, raising her fist. Before she knew what was happening, she punched Paul Neri in the nose, watching the cartilage flatten under her fingers like a hockey stick connecting with a cream puff. Crimson drops of blood spattered the front of her sweatshirt, while hysterical laughter burbled in her throat. "May your Karma descend upon you full force! In the name of the Mother— this is so!"

Tillie grabbed her by the arm and started hauling her out through the gathering crowd as Bethany continued to spew unintelligible curses, her roiling feelings out of control. She turned to see Paul Neri, crumpled on the floor, screaming, blood spurting on the dirty tile mixing with smashed pizza, soggy napkins, and blobs of dried mustard. Someone stepped on his camera.

Chapter 11

*B*ethany wondered about the definition of hysteria. Was it when you wanted to scream until your tongue popped out of your mouth and spittle flew? Was it when you wanted to break everything in sight? Pulverize all physical things until they crumbled like bits of graveyard dust? Or was hysteria a more malevolent thing? Like a black, snaky tendril composed of evil, wicked thoughts that slithered around your throat and slowly reduced the intake of air? Was it this, and more?

Bethany Salem sat in the darkness of her room, her face buried in shaking hands. Was it this?

And more?

Who loves ya, baby . . . that's what Joe had said to her when she saw him last. His husky voice echoed in her mind, and now Nam lay in a hospital room seventy-five miles away. How could this have happened?

Hecate jumped onto the bed, meandering slowly in circles, kneading himself a nest, then plopped indelicately in the mound of covers.

She pulled the hair at her temples and rocked back and forth.

113

Sticky sobs of frustration clung to her throat.

Who had hurt Nam?

Her tearful gaze drifted to the picture of Joe. He smiled at her in that dopey way. Frozen. Caught in time. Living, yet dead. Two candles flickered in the darkened room. A green one dressed with healing oil for Nam. A black one for Joe. She held shaking hands out toward the picture, the candle light dancing on her imploring bare arms.

Who killed you, Joey?

The Cedar Crest Mall had that special smell of new merchandise and negative ion mist from the numerous pounding fountains coated by the strong odor of the food court. Each breath pulled something different to her senses—leather, pizza, plastic, water, egg rolls, overperfumed shoppers, the onion smell of a foot-long sub. She met Tillie halfway across the shiny floor of the upper level, eyes dazzled by designer windows, artificial lighting, and the occasional skylight.

"Nam's going to make it," said Tillie breathlessly. "I talked to her mother right after I phoned you this morning. She's out of surgery, but still unconscious. The doctors say she should wake up soon."

"Does anyone know what happened?" asked Bethany.

Tillie shook her head. "Not until they talk to Nam."

Bethany, jostled by an overzealous shopper, adjusted her purse on her shoulder, realizing her dirty look was lost on the woman's broad back. "I just can't believe it."

"You look like shit," said Tillie as they fell into step beside each other.

"Thanks," said Bethany, "I could say the same about you."

"Yeah, well, I didn't sleep so good last night."

"I wanted to thank you for dragging me out of the bowling alley," said Bethany. "You didn't have to do that."

Tillie smiled. "Hey, what are friends for? Besides, it was worth watching you flatten that pig's nose."

"Is Nick okay?"

Tillie laughed. "Just fine, though I think his pride is hurt. He tried to save the damsel in distress and she morphed into a dragon. He thinks chivalry is dead."

Bethany giggled. They maneuvered around a pack of middle-school kids. "I don't know what came over me. I've never hit anyone before," said Bethany, stopping to stare listlessly at the windows of a novelty gift shop where giant paper pumpkins danced against a background of assorted pale skeletons, green witches, and bloody monsters. "It's a wonder Paul Neri didn't report us to the cops," she said, turning from the window. "Why is it that everyone assumes we're bad just because we chose an alternative religion?"

"Fear," said Tillie.

"It makes me angry!" replied Bethany. "How can people be so cruel?"

Tillie snorted. "Just ask me," she said. "I've been black all my life and it hasn't been easy. I learned when I was just a little kid what discrimination is all about. Welcome to my world."

Bethany looked at her friend with new eyes. She'd never really thought about it before. Tillie was Tillie. To Bethany, color was a moot point. "I don't like it," said Bethany flatly.

"Obviously not," said Tillie, stopping at the Annie-Faye Cookie Counter. "That's some right cross you got there. No wonder you're the star of the girls' hockey team. Look, nobody likes discrimination," continued Tillie as she paid for a giant chocolate-chip cookie. "But, you get through it. You have to if you want to gain anything. Punching people out, though, that's not going to get you anywhere but in deeper trouble." She bit into the cookie, walking away from the counter. "You were lucky this time," she admonished through a mouthful of messy chocolate chips.

Hurrying to catch up, Bethany said, "That guy. Neri. He just wants a story. He doesn't care about Nam or Joe at all."

Tillie turned, an amused smile playing across her lips, offering part of her cookie.

Bethany shook her head.

"Suit yourself. You mean that it just dawned on you that there are lots of people in this world who don't have your best interests at heart? Boy! You are a lamb! Where have you been the last sixteen years of your life, Bethany? In a cocoon?" she asked, waving the half-eaten cookie in the air, crumbs falling like sugared snowflakes.

Bethany thought about that. Where *had* she been? Declaring personal war on nannies and housekeepers, battling the world of crime and justice for her father's attention, running up her dad's charge accounts just so he'd yell at her, talking her father into signing a loan for a car that she couldn't afford, zooming around the house like a spoiled brat the entire time? There were many desperate, starving people in the world, and she hadn't done anything to help them with her new car, fancy clothes, and unlimited credit line. Somehow her personal accomplishments didn't seem all that spectacular after all. The only thing she honestly had a talent for was hockey, and she hadn't really concentrated on that these past few weeks, missing practices and ignoring her team mates. It was a wonder they hadn't kicked her off the team.

She turned and looked at the throngs of people moving up and down the mall. It dawned on her that she knew nothing about the world of humanity. That each person passing her by had their own hopes and fears, challenges and miseries. That each person was an individual with dreams and nightmares. And that there were wolves waiting in a myriad of mazes, prepared to consume the innocent or momentarily stupid. The thought was so heavy she swayed. How many people needed help, but didn't know where to turn?

"Yo! Bethany! Are you okay?" asked Tillie, turning to grab onto Bethany's shoulder.

Bethany hesitated. She felt she should tell Tillie about the dogs at her window. That they wouldn't go away. That maybe, just maybe, they were hunting for her. She couldn't bring herself to say anything. Instead, she said, "Do you think that you and Nick could come over tonight? I know this sounds stupid, but I'd really like to talk about Joe."

"Well, okay, but why don't you call Nick?" asked Tillie. "He's your friend, too," she said, demolishing the last bit of cookie.

Bethany bit her lower lip. "I . . . I just think it would be better if you called," she said.

Tillie put her hand on her hip. "'Fess up, girl-friend. Is there something going on between the two of you?"

Bethany stared at the smooth mall floor. "Of course not!"

"Yeah. Right. And toads are responsible for air traffic control. I watched his reaction last night when that Neri guy went after you. All protective and macho. Tell no lies to these brown eyes."

"He would have done the same for you!" retorted Bethany. "Besides, didn't you see his expression when he realized that Karen was with Todd Lancaster? He's not over her. I don't want some guy who's looking for a quick fix because his girlfriend dumped him." For some strange reason, though, Bethany suddenly wished that Nick did really like her—that it was Bethany Salem Nick truly wanted.

Tillie didn't answer.

Ramona finished loading the silverware in the dishwasher, Hecate circling around her legs. "Ramona will be in the living room while the three of you are in the kitchen," she said, wiping her brown hands on a yellow dish towel. "This is a good place to do homework. *Chaud.* Warm. Roomy. I baked some cookies today. They're in the jar over there," she said, pointing to the big ceramic pig cookie jar with a leering face. "*Lait.* Milk is in the fridge. Wash your glasses out when you are through."

Tillie, Nick, and Bethany looked at each other in dismay. Hecate jumped up on the edge of the kitchen counter, his nose precariously close to the leftover turkey.

"Scat cat!" said Ramona, shooing Hecate off the counter. He turned, uttering a disapproving growl, then stalked out of the room. As if sensing their fear of interruption, Ramona said, "Ramona will not bother you, but Ramona definitely does not wish to go through another broken window episode. Bethany, *mon cherie,* your father called to say he wouldn't be home tonight. Big case. Very sad. Little girl died. Your father thinks she may have been killed by a gang by mistake." She clucked her tongue.

Bethany looked up from the table. "My father never tells me what kind of case he's working on," said Bethany, a surge of pain running through her heart at the thought of a dead little girl. "Why now?" For the first time that she could remember, a flicker of fear traced its way across her throat, building to a tight band around her temples. Was her father in danger?

Ramona shrugged, slapping the towel on the counter. "Perhaps your father feels you are growing up, *mon cherie*. Perhaps he thinks it is time to share certain things with you, or maybe someone told him that it was time his little girl understand what sort of world she is truly living in. Who knows what he thinks, eh?" Her dark eyes sparkled as she stuck her nose up in the air and walked into the living room, her white clothing billowing around her. "He'll be okay, but he is going to do everything he can to close the case. I'll be reading," she said without turning around. "Good book. Ramona likes romance. Please don't disturb Ramona, she's at the good part."

Bethany and Tillie broke into muffled giggles. Nick just shook his head. "She sure is an odd character," he said.

"Man, a dead kid," said Tillie. "Bummer. Gangs." She shivered.

"Yeah," said Bethany, twirling a bit of her thick hair between her fingers. "I mean, I always knew that my dad dealt with bad stuff, but . . . I don't know . . . this sort of seems different."

"Your dad has his case, we have ours," said Tillie resolutely as she pulled a notebook out of her yellow backpack. "We decided to meet tonight so that we could go over everything we know about the last day of Joe's life."

Nick leaned his elbows on the table. "I'm not sure where to start."

"I know this isn't part of the discussion," said Tillie, "or maybe it is," she continued, opening the notebook. "But you better tell your dad about that Paul Neri creep."

Bethany shook her head. "You heard Ramona, he's on a big case. I don't want to bother him. I can take care of Neri."

"I don't know . . ." said Tillie, her lips puckered. "He could escalate from threats to something else since you knocked him silly. I think you should tell your father. This Neri guy wants to use yellow journalism to hurt you and he might take it even further than that."

Bethany sighed. "Okay, when Dad gets home."

Of course, they all knew that Bethany's father wouldn't be home soon.

Nick cleared his throat. "Off the subject, again, but what's the news on Nam?"

"She's awake and out of intensive care," said Tillie. "Her mother says she doesn't know who ran her off the road, but there are some paint scrapes on her car, so the police are investigating. That Neri guy acted like Nam was at death's door just to hurt you,

Bethany. Nam will be home in a day or two. She's complaining because her hospital gown doesn't match her slippers," Tillie finished with a laugh. She twirled a pencil in her hand. "Okay. What do we know about Joe's last day?"

Bethany leaned back in her chair and crossed her arms. "You go first, Nick."

"I saw him throughout the day and he seemed fine. We joked about the seniors graduating and how all the nice babes were leaving." He looked over at Bethany. "Sorry. Just guy talk. Then I saw him that evening. Coach called the football team together to get volunteers to help with a little kids summer athletic program. He helped Coach set up the rosters and we talked about the kinds of activities we would do."

Tillie coughed. Bethany's heart thudded. She took a deep breath. "Did you notice anything at all?" She realized that this was really the first time they'd gotten together to talk about Joe in this way. Sure, they'd talked about his death so much that she was almost sick of it, but this was different. Now they were probing, not hashing out their feelings or trying to make each other feel better. Somehow, this was better. She felt like they were really doing something important.

"What more can you remember, Nick? Think hard," said Bethany.

"Let's see . . . after the meeting, he didn't seem so happy. I thought it was because he didn't like his athletic assignment. But it could have been something else. Now that I think about it, I remember he met some girl outside the locker room. Then I don't know where he went. He shouted something about meeting us all later, and that was it. That's all I know. I left with some of the other guys."

"What girl?" asked Tillie, her pencil poised over hastily scribbled notes.

"I'm not sure," said Nick. "I think it was Vanessa."

"Vanessa Peters?" asked Bethany, a catch in her voice.

"Yeah. That's the one. The prep with the attitude."

Chapter 12

Bethany twisted her hair with her fingers, breaking a few strands, the long dark hairs making white indentations on her skin. "What do you remember, Tillie?"

Tillie shoved the pencil and notebook over to Bethany. "You take the notes, while I try to remember," she said. "Let's see. I was at the school because of band practice. Mr. Shaw, the band leader, wanted to run through the finale one more time before the graduation ceremonies."

She got up from the table and brought over the leering pig cookie jar, digging into his ceramic brains for a cookie. "I went into the bathroom after practice. The one in the stadium, because we practiced there. When I came out, Joe was talking to Karen. They were arguing."

"Arguing?" asked Bethany, her stomach dipping crazily to her toes. "Over what?"

Tillie shook her head. "I don't know because right at that time I came around the corner Joe sort of stepped back. Karen's face was all red. I forgot about it until now. I thought that if it was anything important, Karen would have told us, or at least said something to Nick. Karen always flies off at the least little thing. Sorry, Nick." She bit into the cookie, looking at Nick.

"This is the first I heard of it," he said. "Can you remember anything else?"

Tillie polished off the cookie, offering the jar to the others. "Nope. The next thing I knew, he was dead."

Nick swung his gaze to Bethany. "What do you know about Vanessa Peters? She tried to help you meet your maker with the flick of a Bic. Do you think she has anything to do with Joe's death?"

Bethany swallowed hard. She handed Tillie the notebook and pencil. A shaky breath escaped from her lips. "I think Joe was seeing Vanessa."

Oddly, Nick did not look surprised. Instead, he looked away from her steady gaze. She could do nothing but continue. "But I'm not sure," she said, her words faltering. "I know she had a crush on him because she left some notes in his locker a few times and she called him a lot. He kept telling me it was nothing, and that he'd told her to get lost, but I thought it was so strange that she kept calling him, you know, if there was really nothing to it, and he kept talking to her. Sometimes he would go into the other room with the cordless when she called. And I caught her there a few times—at his house. One time he told me I had no right to tell him who he could be friends with. He actually told me to get out of the room so he could talk to her."

"But I know he really cared for you, Bethany," said Nick gently, yet he refused to look her in the eye. "He talked about you all the time. I'm sure that if something was going on with Vanessa it was just a fling. You know, a sow your oats episode." He played with the edge of the tablecloth.

Bethany got up, stretching her legs. "I think he was messing around with her," she said with conviction as she opened the refrigerator for the milk. Hecate came running in from the living room, his nose aimed for the open refrigerator.

The lights in the house blinked, flashed, and went out.

"What the—?" said Nick, jumping up from the chair, the hard back clattering to the tile floor. Hecate yowled and skittered under the table.

"Stay calm," said Tillie. "It's probably just a power failure. Maybe somebody hit a light pole or something."

Bethany shut the refrigerator door, feeling the whoosh of cold air hit her face in the pitch blackness. That familiar sensation of dread crawled like a half-dead rattlesnake at the pit of her stomach. "I don't like this," she whispered.

"Don't be silly," said Tillie, her voice floating in the dark kitchen. "The lights will be on in a minute."

The lights flicked back on, shocking the retina.

A terrible pounding and a sudden shrill scream echoed through the house, followed by the howling of several dogs. The three friends stood motionless, then scrambled toward the living room, Hecate bolting ahead of them—or, perhaps, away from them.

Bethany called Ramona's name, but she didn't answer. She scurried through the living room, her two friends following close behind. Ramona was not in her favorite chair, but the romance novel lay at the foot of the recliner, pages drifting in the air. The front door hung wide open and a bitter breeze consumed the heat of the house. Light flickered through the dark doorway, splaying patterns of crimson and gold on the hardwood floor. Hecate jumped to his favorite perch on the stairway, peering out into the night, his velvety black ears flattened against his head, the mixture of a hiss and a growl pushing through his sharp teeth.

"What the—?" Bethany stepped through the doorway, calling Ramona's name, as the vision of a burning pile of leaves and grass snared her gaze, the rich smoke spiraling toward the starlit sky. She moved closer, horrified to see the housekeeper's prostrate body not far from the blazing debris. The stench of gasoline cloyed her nostrils as she rushed forward.

"Oh, my God," whispered Tillie, looking at Ramona's still body. "I think she's dead!"

Blood oozed from an open wound on the housekeeper's forehead. Bethany knelt beside her, checking her pulse. "Call an ambulance, Tillie, quick! Ramona! Ramona? Can you hear me?" Ramona's thick eyelids fluttered. "Hang in there. We've called for help." Bethany touched the woman's glistening forehead, drawing her fingers back quickly and sniffing. "Gasoline! Oh, my God, Nick, someone's poured gasoline on her!" The wind rose, picking up burning leaves, sending a macabre dance of sparks and smoke along the picket fence. Bethany bent over Ramona, shielding the woman's body from the hot, falling ashes of the fire. "Put it out!" she screamed. "Get it out! The hose—there, by the side of the house. Turn it on!"

Nick rushed to turn on the water.

"Nick, hurry!"

Ramona's eyelids slowly opened. She coughed. She spoke in French.

"I can't understand you!" said Bethany, trying to keep the hysteria she felt rising in her voice at bay.

"Didn't get in the house, did they?" Ramona muttered, her eyes rolling in her head.

Bethany clutched Ramona's hand. "No one got in the house. Who did this to you?"

The housekeeper groaned. "Ramona didn't . . . see. Heard a noise out front. I . . . I opened the door and stepped out. Shouldn't have stepped over the herbs." She groaned. "Ramona's head hurts. Gasoline burns. My face. My hands. Please, get it off, get it off!"

Bethany remembered something her mother used to say. "Ground and center," she muttered. She stopped and took a deep breath, feeling the power rise within her. Her hands grew warm.

Bethany repeated the incantation her mother taught her. "Hair and hide, flesh and bone, no more pain than any stone. An angel came from the east, bringing frost and fire. In frost, out fire!" She repeated the charm until she thought her voice would give out from her own fear. "Hurry, Nick!" she screamed as he brought the hose. Carefully she washed Ramona's face. The housekeeper sputtered but gave a sigh of relief. Tillie rushed up beside them. "I called emergency services!" she exclaimed, heaving from the run.

Ramona groaned again. Bethany leaned over her, looking up at her friends. "Tillie, can you get a blanket?" Glancing down at the injured woman, she asked, "Is that better, Ramona?"

Ramona whispered a faltering, "*Oui*. Yes."

Tillie ran for the blanket while Bethany tried to staunch the bleeding on the housekeeper's temple with the yards of white fabric from the woman's dress. "Looks like they threw the gasoline in her face," said Bethany. "It doesn't seem to be on the lower part of her dress. We must have scared them away."

Tillie burst out of the house, a blanket flapping behind her. Ramona jerked, coughed, and fell silent. Bethany shook her. No response. Although the light from the sodium streetlight cast only bland bands of white across the yard, Bethany could see that Ramona's skin looked mottled, and her breathing was shallow. "Tillie!" she cried. "Do what I do. Get on the other side of Ramona!"

Tillie scrambled quickly to the other side of the housekeeper.

"Remember what we did in that circle of protection last year?"

Tillie nodded.

"Okay. So we're going to—"

"She's not breathing!" wailed Tillie.

"Yes, she is. It's just real shallow. Come on, Tillie, hang tough."

Her friend nodded, teeth chattering.

"Hold your hands over her, like this," Bethany said, splaying her fingers over Ramona's head, her hands already infusing with heat.

Tillie followed her lead.

"Wait until you feel your hands begin to get warm, then concentrate on pulling energy from the Mother and putting it into Ramona. Ready?"

Tillie nodded, sucking on her lower lip.

"O gracious Lady of the Moon," began Bethany, "Grant to us this simple boon. Healing love and healing luck. I bring the power. I raise it up. Bring the power. Raise it up," she repeated, creating a litany that moved faster and faster. Tillie joined in, their voices low, each repeat of the chant increasing in volume. The heat in Bethany's hands increased despite the bitter cold. It thumped, like a gentle heartbeat. Growing stronger. "I bring the power. I raise it up." she repeated, her eyelids fluttering.

The still point.

She met it.

She wrapped her mind around it.

The energy surged from her fingertips. She could feel her aura expanding. The presence of the Goddess kissing her temple . . .

She didn't hear the sirens.

Didn't see the cops rushing across the yard.

Didn't hear the shouts of concerned paramedics.

There was only the white light.

Somewhere within her mental fog she heard Ramona cough, and say, "I told you. Ramona is sick and tired of being interrupted at the good part!"

Chapter 13

Monday, September 14

Just a bump on the head," said Ramona, straightening her white skirt, then patting the snowy bandage at her temple. "No need to trouble anyone."

Bethany turned the browning sausage and flipped the eggs, watching the whites slide easily in the sizzling butter. Hecate positioned himself right at her big toe, staring passionately at the noisy pan, his nose wiggling sensuously. "Dad was pretty upset when he phoned last night," she said, watching Ramona out of the corner of her eye.

Ramona tilted her head. "It was an upsetting circumstance."

"The Beast of the East just about has him convinced that I should be sent away. She told him that she believes my friends did this to you, and that it would be in my best interests to be confined some place." Bethany plopped four pieces of bread in the toaster.

"Then Ramona will tell him that is not true."

"But you don't really know that, do you, Ramona?" asked Bethany, scooping the eggs onto a plate and adding a few sausages. She plucked two pieces of toast from the toaster and almost tripped over Hecate as she tried to set the plate down in front of Ramona.

"Ramona knows because Ramona knew your mother, and there is no way your mother would have raised a child who would harbor that kind of hatred within her heart." She calmly picked up a fork and began eating her breakfast.

Bethany stared at the woman, open mouthed. The sausage continued to sizzle behind her. "You *knew* my mother?"

Ramona chewed, swallowed, and took a sip of orange juice.

"Ramona?"

The housekeeper forked another piece of sausage into her mouth.

"Ramona!"

"*Oui.* Yes. Ramona knew your mother. We were best friends. Went to high school together."

"But I thought your family lives in New Orleans? My mother was from North Carolina!"

"Ramona has lived just about everywhere. My father was in the military, as was your mother's father. We were best friends for a long time, even after I moved back to Louisiana. We were both army brats. I was there when you were born."

A burning smell touched Bethany's nostrils. She turned quickly, dumping the blackened sausage onto her own plate. "Shoot!" she said. "That means my father knew you before you came to work here."

"It does."

"He called you special, didn't he?"

"He did."

"That's what you meant when you called yourself the keeper."

"Not exactly."

Bethany ran her hands over her face, pulling her thick hair back from her temples with her fingertips as hard as she could. "What do you mean, 'not exactly'?" she asked.

Ramona took the last piece of toast and mopped up a bit of egg. "You have not told your friends, have you?"

Bethany leaned against the counter, still holding onto her hair. "Told them what?"

Ramona licked her fingers. "That your mother trained you, and that she used her skills in investigative journalism. They think everything you know you read out of books or asked the magick shop owners. You have not told them the truth."

Bethany shifted uncomfortably. "How much does my father know?"

Ramona sat back, the wooden chair creaking under her weight. "Everything."

Bethany digested this information. If he knew "everything," as Ramona said, then her father had known all along about Witches' Night Out. About her friends. About many of the things she held private and sacred. She didn't feel comfortable about that. Not at all.

It took her a moment to gather her thoughts. "You're not a nanny."

"No."

"Not a housekeeper?"

"No."

"Then what?"

Ramona took a sip of coffee. "It would appear that Ramona is simply your keeper."

"Sounds like I'm an animal in a pen."

"False drama holds no power," Ramona said, draining her coffee cup.

"Does his girlfriend know?"

"No."

Bethany attempted to bite into a burnt sausage, made a face, and spit it out. She dropped two of the sausages in Hecate's bowl. The cat did a quick dash, grabbed the sausage, and then dropped it, looking at Bethany with distaste. "Now what?" asked Bethany.

Ramona gazed thoughtfully at the empty coffee cup. "Before your mother died, she passed the power to you. I know, because she called me and told me." She held up her hand, warding off Bethany's protests. "She did it while you were sleeping. She knew her time was growing short."

Bethany swallowed hard. "But what about my friends? Are they any less than I?"

"No."

"I don't understand."

"Each comes into his or her power in the way Spirit designed. Some come by it naturally. Some read, study, practice. Others have the power passed to them—like you. This gives you a jump start, but what you do with that power depends on whether it will grow or die. Although the power will flow easier through you, this also means that your choices will be more difficult. Once you have the knowledge, Spirit does not forgive its misuse. What will you do with this power?"

Bethany snorted. "I don't have any power. You're talking nonsense."

Ramona stood slowly. "You performed a healing on me last night. I saw the White Lady descend upon your body. You have the power. Don't be a foolish child and deny it. Ramona is tired. I would like to rest now," she said, ambling out of the kitchen. "If you plan to go anywhere tonight, please leave Ramona a note," she said over her shoulder. "By the way, that red sweater looks good on you. The big boy? Nick? He called you this morning. He wants you and Tillie to meet him in the diner after school."

Bethany stared at the empty kitchen. The clock in the hallway chimed. A sense of foreboding descended upon her. She nervously played with a strand of her hair, running its silky surface slowly across her lips. Was Ramona for real, or did she have her own agenda? Maybe she should talk to her father—ask him to tell her the truth. But what if Ramona was lying? Then her father would make her go away, and if he booted Ramona out, that would give the Beast of the East the perfect excuse to send her away, too. She sighed and grabbed her coat.

Bethany rescued the morning paper that somehow managed to perch in the yew tree. She brushed out a few dead leaves from between the wrinkled pages. The headline caught her eye: Cedar Crest Woman Accosted On Front Lawn. Underneath the bold print was a glaring picture of Ramona on the ground, surrounded by Bethany, Nick, Tillie, and the EMT crew. Paul Neri's byline was underneath the photo. Bethany moaned. Wait until her father got a load of this!

Nick stood halfway down the alley, back resting against the brick wall, his breath seeping into the cold air in white, fuzzy plumes. He wore soft, dark jeans, his blue football jacket with gold and white trim hung open over a flannel shirt. His brown boots were scuffed but expensive. The fading sunset cast eerie purple shadows between the buildings.

Bethany hurried to his side, drawing her coat closely around her, shoving her hands in her pockets. "Tillie went to see Nam," she said. "What's up?"

"We need to talk to Karen," he said. "I thought about it all night. I didn't want to come alone because I don't want her to think that I'm into dating her again. I figured that if we went in together . . . well . . . it would be better. Did you see her in school today?"

Bethany shook her head. "I don't think she was

even there." A stray cat skittered past them, knocking over the lid of a garbage can. The metal sound echoed forlornly against the cold brick walls rising above the alley. They walked around to the front of the diner. The neon tubing over the front door always reminded Bethany of the movie *Grease*. "Maybe she won't be here today," whispered Bethany as they pushed through the revolving glass door.

"Who, Karen or her mother?" asked Nick, looking over her head.

"Both, if we're lucky," said Bethany, following him down the aisle past packed tables and an equally burgeoning counter. The odor of strong coffee and monster burgers, the diner's specialty, assaulted her nose. It felt weird being here. After all, she'd been fired. A place always looked different once you didn't work there anymore. Familiar sounds, smells, and sights almost (but not quite) foreign.

They took a booth near the exit, ordering from a new waitress without incident, neither Karen nor her mother appearing among the hungry customers or busy help. Bethany realized that the smiling girl in the pink uniform was probably her replacement. It was difficult to smile back.

"Looks like this was a bust," said Nick, forking a large mass of French fries dripping with ketchup into his mouth.

Bethany picked at her bacon cheeseburger, mulling over this morning's conversation with Ramona. She opened her mouth to tell Nick about it, then snapped her lips shut just as quickly. Instead, she said, "I think something is very strange with Karen."

Nick pushed his plate away. "No kidding."

Bethany leaned forward. "You don't understand. It's like she's doing and saying one thing, but her heart isn't really in it."

His chameleon eyes turned flat. Ugly. Cold.

Bethany shivered, and she tentatively reached her hand across the table, touching Nick's fingers. His expression changed. Hot. She pulled her hand back quickly, but not soon enough.

"New girlfriend?" Karen snapped, blue eyes filled with hatred as she leaned over the table. "I might have known. I'm gone for less than a week, and here you two are, real cozy together. I'm glad I left you, Nick. I knew you were an unfaithful rat, just like some other guy we used to know." She looked pointedly at Bethany.

Bethany could feel the color draining from her face. What did Karen mean? What other guy? Joe? She hadn't been ready for this kind of confrontation. "You don't understand, Karen," she said softly. "We came here to see you."

"Yeah, and the world revolves on your lies," spat Karen. "Some friend you turned out to be."

Bethany, shocked into silence, said nothing. What was wrong with Karen? How could she twist things around like this?

"Sit down," growled Nick.

Both girls looked at him in surprise.

Karen, her back stiff, ignored Nick's command and turned to Bethany. "You're not even supposed to be in here. Mom fired your sorry carcass. What do you want?"

"I want to know why you're acting so strange," said Bethany, ignoring Karen's dripping sarcasm. "It's just not like you." *Or maybe,* thought Bethany, *you've been this immature all along and I've never noticed.*

"I don't know what you're talking about," said Karen.

Bethany grabbed her arm. "I think you do. I also think that you know something about Joe's death that we don't."

Karen's cheeks flushed the color of her bubble-gum pink uniform and her head jerked, winging that blonde ponytail in a vicious arc. "That's ridiculous!"

Bethany held tightly to her arm. "Don't give me that. What were you and Joe arguing about the night he died? What does Vanessa Peters have to do with all this?"

Karen jerked her arm free, stumbling backwards. "Get out!" she screeched, moving away from them. "Just pick up your check and leave!" She turned and bolted through the double stainless-steel door leading to the kitchen.

"Well, we can't go back in there anymore," said Nick, "considering Karen's father escorted us out of the diner."

Bethany zippered her coat against the cooling September evening. "She's just too strange."

"I'll agree with that. Now what do we do?"

"We keep working on her," said Bethany, rummaging in her pocket for her car keys. "We keep the pressure on. Eventually, she'll crack. I'm convinced now more than ever that she knows something about Joe's death. She might even know something about Nam's accident."

Nick stopped under a streetlight, shaking his head. "She would have said something to me about Joe, Bethany, I'm sure of it. As far as Nam—you saw her. She was all dressed up. She went to that dance with Lancaster. The last thing she had on her mind was hurting Nam."

"You're not convinced. You were the one that wanted to come down here and see her today. What was Karen like on the day of Joe's death? Do you remember?"

Nick ran his hand through his hair. "Oh, man, I don't know. She'd been distant for over a month, sort of. I'd heard rumors—"

"What rumors?"

He shifted his feet, shoulders hunched against the cold. "It doesn't matter. It isn't important. You didn't hear anything, did you?"

Bethany tried to marshal her thoughts. Push away the confusion. "I haven't heard anything," she said slowly. "Is there something I should have heard?"

"No," he said quickly. "That day. The day Joe died, Karen was preoccupied, I guess. I thought it was because of Marissa being such a jerk."

"How is she, your sister?" asked Bethany, moving closer to Nick. "With all that's been happening, I'd forgotten all about her."

Nick let his gaze linger down the street. "Wish *I* could forget her."

"You don't *mean* that! She's all the family you've got."

"She's not any better. Keeps mumbling about cults, curses, our parents, people out to get her—she's majorly screwed in the head. The doctors keep trying different drugs. She just gets crazier. They want to move her to some special facility, and they will, too, if she doesn't snap out of it soon. I don't want her to go. I know how terrible those places can be . . ."

The evening traffic was picking up. A black truck drove by and beeped. Bethany didn't recognize the driver, but Nick must have. He waved half-heartedly. A chilly breeze lifted trash and leaves, swirling them across the gutter. "You see," he said quietly, "my parents were abusive. Oh, they never hit Marissa or anything. Other stuff. Demanding good grades. Never listening to her when she really needed them. Too interested in their money."

A bus trundled by, followed by a dump truck. "Anyway," continued Nick, "she was raped at a college party and my parents refused to listen to her because the guy was some political friend's son. It was terrible. My mother even said that Marissa deserved what she got because she dressed . . . well, sort of tramplike. But that's no excuse!" he said angrily.

Bethany could not believe what she was hearing. How could his mother have been so horrid? A person has the right to wear whatever they want to. It was an excuse. An excuse for violence, pure and simple. "That's just awful!" she sputtered.

Nick rubbed his face. "Marissa went all weird after that. I tried to help her, but I was only fifteen at the time. She stopped talking to them, then went to the drug scene . . ." Those colorless eyes of his bored into hers.

Bethany put her hand on the cold white leather of Nick's sleeve. "I'm so sorry," she said, looking into his eyes. It was a bad move. She knew it before she did it. Too late. The next moment she was in his arms, a strange, sweet fire coursing in her veins. She needed someone so badly right now. His tongue gently touched hers—"No!" she said, breaking free and stepping backwards, her chest heaving.

Nick's eyes filled with pain and Bethany realized that he needed someone just as badly as she did, but was this a good idea? "I've got to go," she said, backing up hurriedly. "I've got to get home."

Chapter 14

Friday, September 18

Karen wasn't in school. She'd been absent all
week. Was she sick? Bethany rummaged in the
depths of her locker, pulling out her English litera-
ture book, shoving the geometry text as far back as
she could. She slammed her locker shut and twirled
the combination. Karen looked fine last Monday afternoon at the diner. Mad, but okay. Bethany sucked
on her lower lip. The bell rang, echoing harshly off
the rows and rows of puke-pink lockers. Shoot! She
was already late for class.

There were a few kids in the hall, rushing (or not
bothering) to get to class. None of them spoke to her.
All of them skirted well around her. As she slipped
into English class, she heard someone behind her
mutter, "Witch! We're gonna get you!" Her head
jerked around, but the hall behind her was empty.
She could not understand this sudden hatred from
her fellow students. Why? Nobody liked Mr. Kuhn.
He was a mass of human sweat with a Napoleon
complex. You'd think they would all be thanking her,
for Goddess' sake! She checked her watch. Five minutes late. She groaned. Mrs. Matthews, dried prune

that she was, did not tolerate tardiness and was known to knock ten points off your current grade for the least little infraction.

Bethany slipped into her seat, ducking her head as Mrs. Matthews glared in her direction. "It appears that some of us haven't as yet learned how to tell time," she sneered, patting the ruffles on her snowy white blouse. "I would have thought, with all your special powers, Bethany, you could just snap your fingers and pop from your locker into the classroom." She walked over to the bank of windows and began pulling down the shades against the dazzling sunlight.

The class giggled.

Bethany could feel her face grow hot, anger and embarrassment clogging her internal voice of reason. She clenched her fingers, trying not to lose her self-control. She swallowed hard. It wasn't helping.

Someone flicked a spitball at her. The old hatred bubbled in her soul. She could feel the tension growing at the edges of her sinus cavities, curling around her eyes.

"I understand your father has considered transferring you to a private school," said Mrs. Matthews, pulling down another shade.

Bethany's eyes widened. How dare this old woman say something like that in front of everyone! It wasn't even true!

Someone in the room cheered.

"That would be such a shame," hissed Mrs.

Matthews, lowering the third shade with a snap. "Our sense of enchantment would be at a loss."

A few of the students shifted uncomfortably in their seats, while others whispered among themselves. Mrs. Matthews moved to the fifth shade, lowering it slowly. "If you will all turn to page 108, we'll be studying the Salem Witch Trials today. I think Bethany will find the part about putting evil to death most interesting. Or, perhaps, like Mary Estes, she'll be struck by lightening."

In the utter silence of the room, someone gasped.

Her temper snapped. Bethany raised her fist and pounded the desk, screaming, "By the deadly skirts of the Dark Goddess, it is you, you old hag, that should be struck down! May your Karma return to you!" At that moment, all the shades roared open, spinning on their metal supports, the one closest to Mrs. Matthews flying from the woman's hand and ripping across her wrinkled cheek. Blood spurted down her white blouse, droplets flicking against the window like sanguine rain.

Mrs. Matthews screamed, but no one moved.

All eyes were on Bethany.

Eric Temple was gaining an unusual reputation among the students. He was a handsome, athletic man in his thirties, liked teaching high school mathematics, and often sided with the student rather than the overactive totalitarianism of the teachers at Cedar Crest High. The crinkled paper on his door read "Acting Principal" in large black, block letters.

Temple looked closely at Bethany. "Let me see your hands, please," he said, his tone neutral.

Bethany held out her hands.

"Turn them over."

She did.

He looked at her long-sleeved, salmon-colored sweater. "Is that what you were wearing first period?"

She nodded.

"You can sit down," he said, leaning back in his chair.

Bethany sat in a wooden chair by the wall.

"My name is Eric Temple. I haven't had you in any of my classes. Your name is Bethany Salem."

Bethany didn't reply, partly because she just couldn't believe this was happening to her again. What would they do this time? Lock her up in a mental hospital? Plant more garbage in her locker?

"Would you mind emptying your purse on my desk?"

Bethany looked at him suspiciously. "I mind," she said, "but I'll do it." She rose slowly, walked over and dumped the contents of her purse across the scarred surface of his wooden desk. Lipstick, pencils, pens, her wallet, and a tampon rolled into a pile of papers. She dug out the brush and plopped it on top, then dropped the leather fringed bag over the mess.

Eric Temple didn't touch anything; instead, he stood and paced the worn carpet of his office, hands in the pockets of his brown pants. He jiggled hidden change. Finally, he said. "Mrs. Matthews claims you slashed her with a knife."

Bethany's jaw dropped open. "That's ridiculous!" she blurted.

"My thought, exactly," said Eric Temple, scratching his chin. "I don't know what is going on around here, or how much culpability lies with you," he said, looking at her closely. "But I tend to believe that Mr. Kuhn made a grave error in judgement."

Bethany didn't utter a peep.

"I also believe that the good-old-boy network at Cedar Crest High is crumbling. You know, people often resist change, and when they are forced to change, sometimes they get mean."

Bethany held her breath.

"And when they get mean, they look for a target. Do you understand what I am saying?"

She exhaled slowly. "Yes."

"Most of the teachers at Cedar Crest are dedicated, intelligent human beings, but like all businesses, we have people here who would be better off somewhere else."

Bethany was trying to follow the thread of this conversation. Was he telling her that she was expelled?

Eric Temple cleared his throat. "There are some teachers at Cedar Crest, and I'm not giving names, you understand, that should have been gone long ago, but because they were friends of Mr. Kuhn's they kept their jobs. Now that he's gone, some of us are hopeful that those people will either retire or choose to leave."

Her heart gave an extra thump. He wasn't talking about her at all!

"In the meantime, however, there's not much we can do. Do you understand me?"

She nodded.

"You can pick up your things from the desk," he said.

Bethany reached forward and grabbed her bag.

Eric Temple sat back down at his desk, an odd smile on his face. "From now on, Bethany Salem, I suggest you watch your back. The town of Cedar Crest isn't exactly a thriving metropolis for meta-physical interests. Many of the people who live here are hiding from strange things like that, hoping such interests self-destruct in the Big Apple. If I were you, I'd cool my . . . ah . . . unusual interests for awhile."

Bethany stood in the doorway and gave him a long look. "Mr. Temple, you're really nice, but you know they won't let you stay here. You're too, well . . . nice."

He shrugged. "But I can make a difference, at least for a little while."

Vanessa the Viper cornered her as soon as she left the principal's office. "Hey, you, Witch girl!" said Vanessa, catching Bethany's shoulder and shoving her against the wall. "Watch your back, sweetheart," she mimicked, and stalked off.

How could she have heard? thought Bethany as she trudged slowly back to her locker. And what really did happen in first period lit? One moment she was sitting in her seat, the next she was standing, shouting, the room in a pandemonium, blood gushing from a deep slash in Mrs. Matthew's face. Did she do that to the woman? Her fingers shook.

Head bent, she walked past several classrooms, the sounds around her eerily muffled. Occasionally she heard the slam of a locker, the echo of footsteps in the stairwell, and the drone of teachers meting out the day's lessons in monotonous boredom behind wooden doors with the customary glass and wire window.

She rounded the corner, her jaw tightening. The door of her locker hung on one hinge, squeaking eerily, as if a ghostly hand played it back and forth. All her books were strewn across the high gloss linoleum, covers ripped, torn pages flicking in the bit of draft. Her shredded backpack hung from the sprinkler system.

A girl's laughter bounced down the deserted hall. Bethany realized it was her own.

Chapter 15

Bethany struggled to hide her disappointment while Ramona bustled around the banging and raucous chatter of the workmen. "I thought Dad was coming home tonight," she said, throwing her books on a table in the hall and trying to figure out what all these people were doing in her house.

Ramona looked at her closely from beneath thick lashes, her dark eyes stern. "Dead little girl is important, *mon cherie.*"

A man in blue overalls with a James Security Company logo on the pocket edged around her, his arms loaded with electrical equipment. Another was busily sweeping the hall, catching plaster and assorted dirt with the edges of the broom.

"What are these guys doing?" asked Bethany, waving her hand at the workmen.

The housekeeper hustled after the man with the broom, brandishing a dust pan. "They are installing a security system in the house. Since your father is called away so often, and we don't understand what is going on here, he decided this would help to keep you safe."

"Why doesn't he just put bars on the windows?" said Bethany angrily, picking up her books and sulking into the dining room.

"He thought of it, but Ramona told him that she refuses to clean the windows if he does that, so I guess this is the next best thing," she said, smiling. "That or buy a dog."

Fear flashed in Bethany's mind. Dogs. Their continued howling at night beneath her window was driving her crazy. Outwardly calm, she said, "Oh, Hecate would really like that, I'm sure." She walked out to the kitchen and dug deep into the depths of the crazed pig cookie jar. Bethany wrinkled her nose when she realized it was empty. Hungry, she opened a cupboard door, scanning the contents. Crackers. A few cans of soup. Rice. Normal stuff.

She banged the door shut and headed for the fridge, nearly tripping over the cat. She reached down and scratched Hecate under the chin. "You knew I was going for the fridge, didn't you?" she asked, opening the door. Hecate merely purred and edged closer. Bethany selected some ham and cheese, throwing the cat a morsel.

Ramona came into the kitchen to empty the dust pan.

"I thought the herbs would keep out the boogieman," said Bethany.

"They do," countered Ramona. "But try to convince your father of that." She handed Bethany a plastic bag stuffed with fragrant, dried plants. "Sprinkle these around the back door, will you?"

"I think you shouldn't leave candles burning in your apartment," said Bethany, finishing off the last of her apple dumpling. She'd noticed the burning candle through Ramona's apartment window when she scattered the herbs around the back door.

"Ramona burns candles all the time," replied the housekeeper.

"Could start a fire," said Bethany. "What are you burning the candle for?"

"*Bougies.* Candles," said Ramona, "plural. Ramona is burning many candles on a fire-safe surface. Don't you worry."

"Okay. Candles. What for?"

"For the dead."

Bethany flexed her fingers, then dragged her hand across the smooth surface of the wooden table. Without looking up, she asked, "Why?"

"Because the dead," explained Ramona, helping herself to another dumpling, "will answer your petitions if you ask nicely." She poured a generous dollop of cream over the pastry.

"They can't," said Bethany slowly. "They're dead."

Ramona laughed, a deep lyrical sound. "The dead, especially those that loved you very much, like to help the living. Oh, they don't make themselves known too often. It certainly would put a lot of religions to shame and scare the bejesus out of people.

Most of them only check in now and then with the living, but if you are really in trouble, you can always petition the dead for assistance."

Bethany's curiosity got the better of her. "How do you talk to the dead?" she asked.

"*Facile.* Easy. You light the candle and say prayers. First to the Mother of All Things, and then you pray for the dead from your heart. You must list those ancestors that went before you. Those that loved you dearly. These prayers and the light of the candle send positive energy to those beyond the veil. This energy helps them. Finally, you petition their assistance. If they choose to help you, then they enhance their own Karma. Ramona has been asking her ancestors for help for many years. They have never let her down." She smiled and took another big bite of dumpling.

Bethany picked at the edge of the table with her fingernails. "Can they do anything?"

"Well. They're not God, you know, they are only dead."

Bethany thought about that for awhile. The hall clock chimed the hour. Hecate swirled around her chair, rubbing his furry black chin on her calf. She reached down and scratched him behind the ears. The thought of being able to actually communicate with her mother or Joe pushed her mind into emotions that she wasn't sure she wanted to face. "Do they talk to you?"

"To Ramona? Sometimes, but not like I'm talking

to you now, though there are some people who say they hold conversations with the dead just like they were right there in front of you. No. They talk to Ramona in different ways. Send her feelings, or impressions, or bits of information that help her to make decisions sometimes. Ramona prays for protection and love every day." She nodded vehemently, her dark eyes large and solemn.

"Do you get what you ask for?"

Ramona forked a piece of dumpling in her mouth. "Well, you don't ask the dead for frivolous things, like a new car or a piece of jewelry. You ask them for help on important things."

"But what about God?"

Ramona dabbed her mouth with a napkin. "You cannot put the dead over the Great Mother, if that's what you mean. They are a part of Her. You must still say your prayers to Her and ask that deity make the path open for the dead to help you."

"Why are you telling me all this?" asked Bethany suspiciously.

Ramona flicked both pudgy hands in the air. "You asked." She flicked a speck of crust off her white shirt. "You don't trust me, do you?"

"No."

Ramona shrugged, polishing off her second dumpling.

By Sunday evening the alarm system had gone off four times. The first time was Bethany's fault. She pushed the button in the hall thinking, in the darkness, it was the light switch. A high-pitched electronic scream emanated through the entire house. Fingers fumbling on the keypad of the phone, she called the security company, barking out their secret code by reading it off the tablet on the table. Hecate scrambled for the family room and streaked under the couch. There was nothing she could do to coax him out, either. By the fourth time, she knew the darned number by heart, rolling her eyes while her father stood sheepishly in the doorway. The cat had permanently ensconced himself under the sofa in the family room.

"Guess it works," he said.

Bethany grumbled, watching Ramona pad up the stairs in her bunny slippers and white terry robe, muttering under her breath in French.

"I didn't expect you home this evening," said Bethany, pulling her own robe closer around her. The hallway clock chimed, the musical notes echoing off the hardwood floor. "How's the case?"

Her father trudged across the living room, plopping down in one of the overstuffed chairs. "Lousy."

"How's Angela?"

Her father's face brightened and Bethany's heart sank. He was still gripped by middle-aged insanity, cop or not. "She's got herself a big case. All in a bluster. That woman will conquer the country to get a not guilty verdict." He laughed. "Such enthusiasm," he said, kicking off his shoes.

"How come you came home?" asked Bethany.

Her father ran his hands through his graying hair. "I wanted to tell you something, and I felt it was better if we could sit down and talk about it."

Bethany stepped forward, gripping the back of the recliner. When someone tells you they want to say something to your face, it usually isn't something you want to hear, and she was sure she didn't want to listen to whatever her father had to say.

"Angela and I have chosen a date for our marriage," he said, a loopy grin expanding his mouth to clown proportions. "We'd like to do it Christmas day."

Bethany sat in Nick's truck after school, watching the students of Cedar Crest High swarm across the wet macadam and roar out onto the main road.

"We've got to talk," said Nick, staring through rain-soaked windshield, dirty drops of water oozing across the glass.

"I'm listening," said Bethany, fearful that he would tell her he didn't like her anymore. That he was quitting Witches' Night Out. That he was leaving her alone to face the problem of Joe's death.

"Karen called me."

"What did she want?" Bethany's throat tightened. It was stuffy in the cab of the truck.

Nick fidgeted with the steering wheel. "I know why she hasn't been in school."

"Is she sick?"

He shook his head, his chin trembling. "No. No, she's not exactly sick."

Bethany clutched her purse, waiting for the worst. Waiting to be dumped before she'd ever been picked up.

"She's pregnant."

Bethany's purse dropped to the floor of the cab. "What?"

"It isn't mine."

"Oh, man!" said Bethany, her mouth refusing to close properly. When she finally regained her senses, she asked, "Then whose is it?"

"She won't tell me."

"Then what's she going to do?"

He shrugged. "I don't know. She wants to tell her parents that I'm the father."

"You're kidding!" said Bethany. "How could she *do* that? How could she *ask* you such a thing?"

Nick rubbed his face with his hands so hard that he pulled the skin in amazing shapes. Bethany's stomach twisted in knots.

Nick looked at her, his face pale and drawn. "My sister is *really* sick. I've had to take care of everything. Pay the bills. Make sure the nurse takes care of her right. My grades are going down. I'm afraid I won't be able to get into college, and if Marissa stays the same, there won't be enough money . . ." He looked up at her, those chameleon eyes filled with tears. "I don't know what to do." He pounded the steering wheel of the truck.

Bethany felt anger rumble at the base of her spine, threatening to explode and rip her head off. How could Karen even suggest such a thing? She got herself into trouble, and now she wanted to ruin Nick's life, too. How could she be so unfair?

Just when Bethany thought she might be able to have feelings for someone again, Karen slithered in and whisked it all away.

She hated.

O Goddess, *how* she hated!

Chapter 16

Instead of getting together at her house on Thursday, Tillie and Bethany visited Nam at home. Nick hadn't spoken to any of them all week. Nam's mother greeted the girls with smiles and hugs. "Since Nam's accident, we've had lots of time to talk. I realize that her father and I were hasty in our decisions, especially after we talked to your father's . . . well, er . . . friend, Angela. Did your father tell you, Bethany, that the school offered to settle out of court?"

Bethany shook her head, but Tillie whispered, "To the tune of several thousand dollars. My father is donating his portion to the new church they're building outside of town. It's supposed to be for all faiths. He's real excited. He said that the Goddess was allowed in his church anytime." She giggled.

"I haven't talked to my father about that," said Bethany lamely.

The woman's face beamed. "Nam's father and I will bring our family over from China with our money," she said shyly. "I cannot wait to see my children!" she exclaimed, tears wavering in her eyes.

160

"What is your father going to do with the portion of his settlement? Oh, that's right. You said you haven't spoken to him about it. Silly me." She waved a delicate hand in the air, blinking her eyes rapidly.

With Nam's parents' permission, they did a healing ceremony. Nam's mother even helped.

On Friday evening, Bethany wandered listlessly around her bedroom. She took the picture of Joe off her dresser and removed the wreath from the gilded frame, throwing it in the trash. She sat on her bed, running her hands over the smooth surface of the glass. It was cool and silky to the touch.

"If you could talk," said Bethany to the picture, "then why haven't you told me who killed you?"

The clock in the hall chimed the hour, but other than that, there was no answer. She set the picture up on her bureau. "Ramona said that I should say prayers to deity and then I should light a candle for you, and ask you to help me," she said to the picture.

Joe's image didn't answer. It just kept smiling at her in that dorky way that she loved so much. Her breath hitched in her chest. "I'm going crazy," she said aloud. "I'm talking to the picture of a dead person, expecting it to talk back. Which it won't, will you?"

No reply.

She sighed. "If I was really any good at this Witch stuff, you would be talking to me nonstop."

Silence.

Bethany circled the room, her stockinged feet stomping on the carpet. She hugged herself. Nick hadn't talked to her in private since the news about Karen. It was as if he purposefully avoided her unless there were other people around. She couldn't call his house because he let the answering machine pick up, and if Marissa would hear she'd go into one of her episodes.

Bethany plopped back down on the bed. Hecate scampered into the room, took a flying leap and landed on top of a down pillow. Attack cat trounces fluffy foe, thought Bethany idly, tracing the pattern of the colorful quilt with her finger. She could feel that familiar pulsing in her hands, that tingling in her fingertips, as if her body was willing her to do magick when her mind had not decided upon it.

"Okay," she said to Hecate. "If I try and fail, nobody will know, right?"

The cat looked at her through slanted eyes, a loud, monotonous rumble emanating from the depths of the pillow.

She sat cross-legged in front of Joe's picture, a purple candle whispering in the stillness, the flame shooting up three inches, unwavering now. Hecate jumped down on the carpeted floor, padded over to the photograph, sniffed, and edged near the candle, one paw extended to bat the flame. "Don't do that!" Bethany reprimanded, shoving the cat out of the way. Hecate crouched on his haunches and hissed.

"Bad kitty!" said Bethany, shaking her finger at him, which he immediately pounced upon. She jerked her hand away and the cat rolled playfully under the bed, contenting himself to attack the dust ruffle. "I can't believe I ever assumed you could be a familiar," said Bethany in a disgusted voice. "I'd get more action out of a toad."

Ignoring the cat, Bethany opened her arms, tilting her head toward the ceiling, her eyes watching the delicate dance of light and shadow on the white walls. "O gracious Lady of the Moon, grant to me this special boon. Grant me strength, power, and humility. Please, let the words of the dead come forth to me."

A bang somewhere in the depths of the house. Ramona had gone out, she was sure of it. She'd watched the woman get in a taxi, and waited until the yellow vehicle rumbled around the corner. Imagination? The wind? A loose shutter? Except the house had no shutters. Bethany shivered.

The candlelight wavered, throwing a soft halo around the picture of Joe's head. Bethany smiled thinly. She was crazy, that's what she was. Wanting and thinking she could bring back the dead. Total nonsense. Yet she persisted, holding her hands out as if she expected Joe to plop some trinket in her palm. Hecate continued to roll around under the bed, worrying a loose edge in the carpet. At least, with the cat there, she knew there were no monsters under the bed—except Hecate, of course.

Okay. She'd said a prayer to the Goddess. Now what? Oh, a prayer for the dead. She didn't know any so she supposed she'd just have to make one up. "Great Mother, She who is the crowned Queen of the Universe—Holy Mother, I send positive energy to those who have gone before me. My grandparents, my mother, and Joe. Bless them and keep them. Show them your special gifts. Teach them so that they may reincarnate in places of peace and tranquility, where their spirits may grow and shed light upon the darkness of men's evil." Her litany continued, words pouring from her soul. When she was finished, she wasn't even sure what she'd said, but she guessed it didn't really matter. Ramona said she should speak from the heart, so that's what she'd done. Hecate growled softly from somewhere across the room.

Now, the hard part. She could feel her throat constricting, the tears welling up in her eyes. She knew it was silly, but she felt like Joe was in the room, standing right beside her, telling her not to worry, that he still loved her. That he cared.

Her lower lip quivered. "Joe? Joe, this is Bethany," she said, looking at the picture through swimming eyes. "I miss you very much." She almost broke down, then. Almost. "I'm so sorry about the accident," she went on. "They say that you hit that tree because you were going too fast. But, see . . . I know you. You were a very careful driver. I think someone killed you on purpose. Made you turn into that tree.

I'm so sure I'd stake my life on it." She took a deep breath. "And maybe I have. I did a ritual, Joe, with the others. A ritual to catch your killer, but it's not working, or . . . at least I don't think it is. So many crazy things have happened. And now there are big black dogs wailing under my window every night, but no one except Ramona hears them. I'm afraid. So very afraid! My dad is going to marry this evil woman. He wants to send me away. I don't want to go!" she wailed.

The sobs wracked her body and it took a moment to get herself under control. "Anyway," she hiccuped. "Help me get the person who did this to you." Anger welled in her, replacing the tears. "Help me avenge your death!"

The candle guttered.

The cat jumped out from beneath the bed, the legs of a spider sticking out of his mouth.

The alarm tripped.

And she thought she heard someone whisper, "Who loves ya, baby?"

Her first instinct was to bolt, but she froze for just a second, her eyes roving around the room. Nothing. Wincing from the shrill scream of the alarm, she reached for the phone, thinking to call the alarm company, but halfway through the number she realized that the alarm may actually be legitimate. Her hand wavered over the keypad as her head turned toward the doorway of her room.

Marissa stood there, blood dripping down her

left arm, plopping softly on the carpet, her eyes wild, her hair matted and filthy.

Hecate yowled, the dead spider still curled in his mouth.

Marissa lifted her right arm, her hip leaning slightly against the doorway. The candlelight glinted off the long steel blade of a hunting knife. "We've all got to die sometime," screamed Marissa over the blaring of the alarm. A wild moan escaped from her swollen lips. She licked them quickly, her legs wobbling.

Bethany gasped.

The alarm continued to blare.

Marissa raised the knife slowly, as if she was about to charge. Her eyes opened wider as if in surprise. "Joe," was all she said.

And plunged the knife deep into her own chest.

The eerie wail of dogs merged with the jarring sound of the alarm.

The consternation was unbelievable. People were everywhere—the Cedar Crest police, the county coroner, EMT's, neighbors, television and newspaper reporters—even the generally curious flocking like bats at a feeding frenzy. Bethany sat among it all, huddled in her quilt on the family room sofa, a female police officer by her side. Paul Neri, the photographer, had tried to muscle in the front door, but one of the officers grabbed him and hustled the pudgy photographer out to his car. Ramona had not returned, her father was on a stakeout, and the Beast of the East had been called back to court for a late-night verdict.

She'd never felt so incredibly alone.

Chapter 17

"I don't know how she got in," sobbed Bethany, clutching the edge of the quilt, sodden with her tears.

Carl Salem sat beside Bethany, taking her into his arms. He nodded at the female officer, who threw him a thin smile and left the room. "It looks like she broke the glass pane on the front door and let herself in. The alarm went off, which alerted the security company. They were here in less than five minutes."

"Not soon enough," said Bethany, hiccuping away a sob.

Hecate, tired of all the emotion, sidled over to the window, peering out into the blackness of the night.

"Why would Marissa want to kill you, Bethany? Have you done something I should know about?"

Bethany felt like laughing. What could her father possibly think that she would do to someone? She felt like she was going to throw up. "I haven't done anything!" she said through clenched teeth. "I don't understand it! And she didn't hurt me, she killed *herself!*"

Carl Salem rolled his shoulders, bending his head to one side as if he was in pain. "Did she say anything to you?"

"I'm . . . I'm not sure," said Bethany, pawing at the quilt. "The alarm was so loud . . . I think she said, 'We've all got to die, sometime,' but it happened so fast . . . I'm just not sure." She refused to tell her father that she thought Marissa called out Joe's name. After all, she could have heard her wrong. It could have been "no," not "Joe".

"Where is Ramona?" he asked angrily.

"I don't know. She left in a taxi hours ago. I'm not sure what time. I saw her leave from my bedroom window."

His cheeks flushed. "She didn't tell you she was going somewhere?"

"No."

"And you were all alone in the house? No one else was here?"

"You should know that," snapped Bethany.

The silence lengthened between them. This was the worst night of her life and she felt like her father wasn't really in the body of the man sitting beside her. What had happened to him? His face, filled with shadows and a twenty-four-hour growth of whiskers, looked exhausted and ancient. Cold pools of sapphire gray replaced the normal jaunty fire in his eyes.

"How are we going to tell Nick?" asked Bethany, fresh tears coursing down her cheeks.

Her father's eyes softened for a moment. "I'm going over there in a few moments."

"I want to come," said Bethany, dropping her feet to the floor, struggling with the quilt.

"No."

"Why not? I should be there!"

He shook his head. "This is police business. I'm out of my jurisdiction, but they're going to let me handle it. Tillie and her parents are on their way over here. They're going to stay with you until I get back. Then we'll go to my apartment in the city."

"I want to stay here!"

Carl Salem's jaw hardened. "That's impossible. We won't be able to stay here for at least two or three days. Your room . . ." he winced. "After the police finish their investigation, we'll have to call in a professional cleaning team. You simply cannot stay here."

"Then I'll stay in Ramona's apartment," said Bethany.

"Nothing doing. I don't know what's going on around here, Bethany, but I can't do my job and worry about you."

"Your job!" wailed Bethany. "Who cares about your job!"

He ran his hands through his hair. "I almost had him tonight. Had him and lost him."

"Had who?"

"The case I was working on. The man who killed the little girl."

Guilt rushed over Bethany on the heels of her

anger. It wasn't her fault that Marissa decided to rip open her chest in Bethany's bedroom, but it was within her power to treat her father fairly, even if he didn't realize he was not giving her the same favor. However, she would not allow him to take her to the city, into the waiting fangs of Angela. Not a chance.

"I thought you said the killing was gang related."

"I thought it was," said her father, "but I got a tip..."

"I want to stay in Ramona's apartment," she said firmly. "I don't want to be ripped out of school."

"I strongly feel that taking you back to the city would be best," he said. "You aren't winning any popularity contests at school, anyway. Let's face it, in the four and a half years we've been here, you've been an outcast. Do you think I've missed that fact? I should think you would want to go somewhere else. Start over fresh. I could look for another place. Sell this house. Find a town that's a little more progressive." He rubbed the bridge of his nose. "It appears that small doesn't mean safe."

Bethany shoved her lower lip out stubbornly. "You once told me not to make a habit of running away. You were right. I want to know *why* Marissa committed suicide in our house. I want to know *why* Joe was killed."

Carl Salem angrily ran his fingers along the worn collar of his shirt. "How many times have I told you, Bethany, that Joe's accident was just that—a sad, unfortunate, terrible accident. No one tried to kill him.

He was driving too fast. There was a heavy rain storm, for pity's sake! Did you know that there were twelve separate accidents in the county that night because of the weather, and five of them ended up in fatalities? That's it. Call it a freak of nature. Call it an act of God. Call it anything but murder! You've got to get over his death and get on with your life!"

Bethany crossed her arms tightly, shoving her tongue behind her front lip and pushing hard.

"As far as Marissa is concerned, the woman was being treated for a mental condition. She fixated on you. I'm not sure why, but she did. Unfortunate, but who knows what lurks in the twisted minds of people? I see things everyday that I can't explain away." He shook his head. "She wasn't right in the head for months, anyway. She should have been in a hospital," he said, eyes beginning that slow burn Bethany knew so well. Internally, she recoiled, knowing that she was going to have to put up quite an argument to convince him of anything right now. "You're coming back to the city with me!" said her father, with that tone of finality she dreaded.

Bethany pounded the quilt with her fists. "No! No, no, no! I'm sixteen. I'm old enough to make some decisions about my life. I do *not* want to go back to New York City!" She realized how childish she must look. If she was going to yap about being grown up, she better act like it. "I'm sorry," she said. "It's just that if I go, I'll feel like I left . . . well . . . like a coward."

He father rose, towering over her. "We'll talk about it when I get back. I've got a job to do."

Bethany had answered so many questions she felt dizzy. She huddled with Tillie on the sofa, eating cookies and drinking hot chocolate brought by Tillie's mother. Tillie's parents sat opposite them on the loveseat. A dull silence pervaded the room and now and then, the adults would murmur to each other. The hall clock chimed—a sad, desolate sound.

Ramona and Bethany's father returned at the same time, their presence accentuated by the angry roar of her father and Ramona's equally strong retorts drifting from the front hallway.

"And I am to know," yelled Ramona, "exactly when a crazy woman is going to break into the house?" A stream of French spewed from the hallway, bouncing off the windows in the family room.

Tillie's parents looked at one another with raised eyebrows. Bethany slid further under her quilt. This was embarrassing.

"No matter what you think, Ramona is *not* God!" she shouted, "and I have a right to take at least one evening off!" Another flurry of French. "I have watched your daughter like she was a bug under a glass for three weeks! *Oui!* Yes! Count them on my fingers. *Un. Deux. Trois.* Three full weeks! Regardless of what you think, you are Ramona's employer and she *does* have a life! I don't remember throwing marriage vows into the bargain and Ramona does *not* have to tell you where she went or what she did there! You are hardly ever home, and when you are, you bring that slut into the house and parade her in front of your daughter. You are a fool, Mr. Salem. The woman is only after your money. You don't really think she loves you? A working cop? A man almost twice her age? Get your head out of the clouds!" she screamed, each word raising in volume until Bethany thought the plaster would fly from the walls. "Felicity, your dead wife, would be horrified," Ramona pronounced, a viscous edge to her voice.

There was a terrible, deadening silence.

Tillie's eyes widened, her mouth crimped in a startled slash. Her parents looked at each other, as if frozen in time. Tillie's mother leaned forward. "Are there one or two women out there?"

"I'll explain it later," Tillie whispered back.

Bethany felt like her limbs were carved in marble.

Tillie's parents stood up, looking at each other. "Tillie," said her mother, "I think that it's time we go." She reached over and grabbed Bethany's hand. "You know, sweetheart, you can always come and stay with us. We'd love to have you."

Bethany felt her body melt back to normal. "That's very kind of you," she said hoarsely, "but I think we have some things to work out here, first."

Tillie's mother smiled. "You know," she said, looking strangely at Bethany, "you really should do something about those dogs wandering around. I saw four big black ones at the side of your house when we drove up. Are they yours?"

Bethany gripped the quilt, her knuckles turning white. "Dogs?" was all she could utter.

The older woman smiled, a touch of sympathy in her eyes. She bent over and whispered in Bethany's ear. "Men are such gullible creatures sometimes. Don't worry, he'll wake up."

Bethany let out a delicate snort, releasing her clawlike grip on the quilt.

Chapter 18

Bethany didn't know how Ramona pulled it off, but her father relented and let her stay in the apartment over the garage. Not so good—he drove back to the city without saying goodbye. Now she sat on Ramona's living room floor, surrounded by tables packed with books, candles, herbs, oils, and all manner of exotic-smelling stuff. It was like the best occult emporium in the world complete with a basket of black chicken feathers.

"If my dad knew what this place looked like," said Bethany, her eyes roving from the huge statue of Mary to the painting of Buddha on the wall, "he would never have let me stay with you."

Ramona threw her a pillow and a blanket. "Ramona is not giving up her bed. You can have the couch."

Bethany looked at a dried bird foot on the end table by the sofa, inches from where her head would go, and shuddered. "Where did you go tonight?" she asked, putting her pillow at the opposite end.

"None of your business," said Ramona. "If you get cold, there is an extra blanket in the hall closet. Ramona is sorry she wasn't there when you needed her. Ramona feels very bad about the whole awful affair."

Bethany ran her fingers through her thick hair. "It's not your fault. It isn't my fault, although I'm sure Angela will turn it around somehow and use it against us."

Ramona put the tea kettle on the electric burner, then went about pouring various herbs from a set of clear canisters on the counter into a bowl. She used a pestle to gently crush the dried leaves. The circular motion of her wrist had a soothing effect. Bethany yawned.

"Why do you think she did it?" asked Bethany, curling her legs underneath her.

"*Qui?* Who?"

"Marissa. Why do you think she went to the trouble of breaking into the house and then stabbing herself?"

The pestle made a soft, singing sound as Ramona continued to stir the herbs. "Magick and ritual can do wondrous things. They can bring harmony out of chaos. Magick and ritual, after all, are only a means of balance."

Hecate peeked around the edge of the couch, sniffed at the crow's foot and batted at the black ribbon hanging from one frozen bird claw.

"What's that supposed to mean?" asked Bethany. "And what does that have to do with Marissa?"

The tea kettle began to whistle, shooting steam at the slowly revolving ceiling fan. Ramona reached over and removed the kettle, the whistle dying. She didn't answer.

Bethany tucked her hair behind her ears. "Just like the name in the freezer, your folk magick doesn't really work. And what about those protection herbs? They didn't work. Magick isn't real."

Ramona did not look up from the bowl of herbs. "But it is. All magick takes its good time, especially when one is just learning."

"Excuse me?" asked Bethany, snapping her wrist in the air. "The woman cut her heart out in my bedroom right in front of my face."

"Did you die?" asked Ramona.

"Well, no."

"Did the woman harm you?"

"I'll be psychologically dysfunctional for life," declared Bethany.

"Into every life a little rain must fall. We all carry scars," replied Ramona. "Do you think Marissa was a bad woman?"

Bethany considered that question. Finally, she said, "I really don't know."

Ramona shrugged and tapped some of the herbs into two tea balls. "Then everything we have done so far has worked. You are in one piece."

"Thank you for small favors," muttered Bethany. She thought Ramona's reasoning might be a bit faulty, but she didn't know how to argue the point.

The housekeeper set the tea balls in heavy mugs, then poured the steaming water over them. "Did you ever think that many of the things happening to you over the past several weeks are a direct result of your magick and ritual?"

Bethany's could feel her guard snap to attention. "What do you mean?" She felt fear in her gut. What if it was her fault that Marissa committed suicide? Is that what Ramona was trying to get at? She could feel the warmth drain from her cheeks. If that was so, she would never, ever touch anything magickal again!

Ramona strained the tea through white cheese-cloth into fresh mugs, carrying one over to Bethany.

"What's in this?" asked Bethany, sniffing cautiously.

"Something to make you sleep."

"I don't want to sleep," said Bethany, handing the mug back. "And I don't take drugs."

Ramona cocked her chin to the left, raising an eyebrow, but did not move to take the mug. "Ramona does not believe in drugs either. It's only chamomile, bee's honey, and a few other herbs not worth mentioning."

Tillie met her at the double glass doors of the school. "I didn't think you'd come today," she said as several kids passed by them, intent on getting to homeroom before the bell rang.

Bethany shifted her books on her arm. "My dad wanted me to stay home, but I'd just be sitting in Ramona's apartment, looking at all the weird stuff she's got in there."

Tillie raised an eyebrow.

"Don't ask," said Bethany, as someone jostled her hard. She looked up to see Vanessa and her friends forming a circle around them, angry expressions on their faces.

"There's the Witch girl!" taunted Vanessa. "Do you know she killed Nick's sister?"

Another girl, that cheerleader with the fox-red hair, spat at Bethany, the saliva hitting her square in the chest, dripping down the front of her sun-yellow sweater. The other girls laughed. Bethany looked up, feeling hatred engulf her body.

"What are you gonna do," asked someone, "curse us, too?"

"We're going to take care of you," whispered Vanessa, her sleek, seductive face turning into a masque of loathing. "You're gonna die just like Joey and Marissa!"

Tillie stepped forward, but Bethany held her back. "Not now," she said softly. "Not now."

"What do you know about Joe's death?" challenged Bethany, stepping closer to Vanessa.

The other girl took a small step backwards. "Isn't that a question *you* should be answering?" she asked hotly.

Bethany noticed a slight tremor under Vanessa's eyes. "I think you had something to do with it, that's what I think!" said Bethany, low and slow. "I heard you were arguing with him the night he died. Someone saw you outside of the stadium."

Vanessa's breath hitched, her lower lip trembled. "That's not true!"

Bethany stepped closer. "But it is, isn't it, Vanessa? What were you arguing about? You were chasing after Joe like a cat in heat. I know. Remember? You called him all the time. Always trying to horn in on our relationship. Were you angry that he didn't want to see you any more?"

Vanessa's nostrils flared. "That slut, Karen! That's why you killed Joe!"

"Don't go there," warned Tillie, her dark eyes darting from Vanessa to Bethany nervously.

"What does Karen have to do with this?" asked Bethany. "I thought she was a friend of yours?"

"Don't act so stupid!" hissed Vanessa.

"Shut up, Vanessa!" shouted Tillie. "Drop it!" Tillie was now clearly alarmed.

Vanessa shot an amused glance at Tillie. "You know. See! Tillie knows."

Bethany looked questioningly at her friend.

Tillie's dark eyes swam with tears. "Shut up, Vanessa. She doesn't know!"

"Like heck I will," said Vanessa, squaring her shoulders and flicking coiffed hair with high-gloss nails.

"What is she talking about?" asked Bethany, trying to keep the desperation out of her voice. "What is she saying?"

Tillie fixed her eyes on the slick linoleum hallway.

A crowd began to gather around them, with several seniors on the fringes, giving the others knowing looks.

"It's the oldest story in the book," said Vanessa, warming to her audience. "The green-eyed monster. That's why you tried to run Joe off the road, and succeeded!" she shouted. "Don't try to fake your way out of this. Your little Witch group thinks you're so cool. But we know the truth! Karen told us all about it! Even one of your own members couldn't trust you. She told us how you curse people. How you make people sick. We heard about what you did to Mrs. Matthews—cutting her face open with your magick! And how you did some love spell on Karen."

The other girls nodded.

"That's absurd!" said Bethany. "I've never done a love spell in my life."

Vanessa snorted. "No, you just hex people. See?" She looked up at her audience. "She admits it!"

The crowd emitted a low, malicious rumble.

"Maybe the law can't do anything about you, Bethany Salem," said the redhead, "but we can. Just watch your back."

"That's right," said Vanessa. "Everybody in the whole school knows. We think it's disgusting how you were walking around, mooning over Joe, when you knew all along that he was the father of Karen's baby and caused his death. You are one sick piece of trash."

Tillie bowed her head and groaned.

Bethany felt as if someone had just shot her with a thousand hot needles. She wavered, wondering if her feet were still beneath her. "Wh-what?" she croaked, praying to the Goddess that what she just heard wasn't true. It was a terrible, horrible rumor. Nothing more. Nick was the father of . . . but, no . . . he wasn't. "That's not true," she gasped, "it couldn't *possibly* be true."

"As sure as I'm standing here!" announced Vanessa.

Bethany looked at Tillie, her mouth gaping. "You *knew?* You knew all along and you didn't *tell* me?"

Tillie took a step back, sputtering, her dark eyes filled with shameful tears.

"How could you *not* tell me?" she screamed. Bethany tore away from the group, running out the glass doors and down the cement steps. Some of her books fell out of her arms. She didn't stop to pick them up. She just wanted to run. Run away. She could hear Tillie calling her name behind her, but she didn't stop.

Bethany bolted to her car, hit the automatic lock, threw it into gear and tore out of the lot, nearly hitting Tillie, surrounded by the cheerleaders, panic on their faces. They scattered like shrapnel from a misfired bomb.

She didn't care if she mowed them all down!

Chapter 19

Hatred slid into her heart like ragged silk across an open wound. She pressed on the accelerator, whizzing around Slate Hill Road, scattering gravel, dead leaves, and debris. Faster! How could they have kept this a secret from her? How could she have been so blind?

Faster. The needle twitched at seventy miles per hour. The car responded, its precision manufacturing kicking in.

Who knew? Nick? Did he know? He must have. She remembered standing on the street corner with him, the traffic whizzing by. He wanted to know then if she'd heard any rumors. Nam? She didn't think so, but maybe . . . she'd been so pensive. And Tillie? When had she found out? The rear end of the Camaro fishtailed slightly as she made a hard right onto Orr Bank Road, the vehicle surging into eighty miles per hour.

Bethany tried to blink away the tears, running the back of her hand hard over her eyes, skewing her vision for a moment. They'd all known! Every one of them! How many girls had Joe been with? Obviously Karen. Vanessa? Most likely. Eighty-five miles per hour. She swerved to miss a skinny yellow cat.

Were there others? Marissa? Oh, Goddess, no! Not *her*? She was so old! At least twenty. But she had called his name right before she killed herself . . . and Joe used to spend a lot of time over at Nick's house—*Get hold of yourself, Bethany!* They were friends. That's all just friends. But he'd not been "just" friends with Karen, now, had he?

She spun the wheel hard, the car flying over several bumps in the road, settling out to ninety miles per hour on the straightaway of Whiskey Springs Road, slowing a bit to take the Y intersection leading off to Barr's, flying past the drive-in. Ramming her foot on the brake. The car bucking, skidding on wet leaves and loose gravel, slowing to squealing stop. She backed up the car. Slammed on the brakes.

She threw the car into gear, spinning out and back the way she'd come. At the outskirts of Cedar Crest, she began to reduce her speed, her anger spent on terrifying curves and blood-curdling shoots through underpasses and over Raymond's Bridge. She'd taken the turn into town on two wheels. *What am I doing?* she thought as the car skittered toward an embankment, then straightened out onto the main road. She coasted into the parking lot of the diner, where a large red and white sign buckled in a slight breeze, red, white, and blue pennants flicking in the sunlight. "Under new management," she read, as if the words came straight from the Holy Bible.

Slowly, she backed up the cherry red Camaro, following the speed limit to the opposite edge of town, to the Cedar Crest Pines Trailer Park. She drifted past Karen's double-wide trailer. Braked. Stopped. The broken screen door slapped listlessly in the chill September breeze. A crow circled overhead, a long, forlorn scream dropping from its bill like so many darts on a battered board. Hollow black windows stared back at her.

Empty.

Bethany leaned over the steering wheel and wept.

It was dark and cold. Bethany leaned against her mother's gravestone, her eyes swollen, her lips cracked and bleeding from hours of crying in the cold air. She rocked herself ceaselessly. Back and forth. Back and forth. She wanted to cry, but her body wouldn't cooperate. She felt bruised inside from the wracking sobs that shook her body for hours. Now, she rocked. And stared.

"I thought I'd find you here," said Tillie, reaching down and placing a warm hand on Bethany's icy cheek.

Bethany rocked.

"I'm sorry I didn't tell you. I'd hoped the rumors weren't true. I'm so sorry."

Bethany curled her arms tighter around her body, rocking, rocking, rocking. It was as if Tillie was talking to her from a very deep cave beneath the surface of the earth.

Tillie kicked a loose stone, the toe of her sneaker dragging across gravel and grass. "I was hoping that you would never find out. I really thought they were just nasty rumors."

Bethany fixed glazed eyes on a cold world.

Rocking.

"The police have matched the dent and the paint left on Nam's car to Marissa's blue Toyota. They still don't know why she tried to run Nam off the road, or why she killed herself in your house. It was in the papers this evening."

Mist began to creep across the graveyard, twist around the headstones, and dance in the growing light of the waxing moon.

Tillie slapped her hands against the fluffy down of her coat and shivered. "Ramona is worried about you. She's been calling my house all afternoon."

Bethany continued to rock.

Tillie looked around the graveyard, her dark eyes wide and sad. "Vanessa's real sorry. So are the other girls. I had to deck her first, though, to get her to listen."

Bethany paused.

"I assume you know that Karen's family pulled out of here like the devil was after them," said Tillie.

An owl hooted. The flap of wings. A swoop. Silence. Bethany began to rock again.

"Joe's still dead, you know," continued Tillie, a note of desperation in her voice. "And we still don't know who killed him," she said, looking uncomfortably over her shoulder in response to the cracking of a twig nearby. "Come on, Bethany. We've got to go."

Bethany stopped rocking. "Why?"

"Just because he was seeing other girls doesn't mean that he should have been killed. So he lied. So he cheated. He was still a human being, and somebody just decided to take his life." She snapped her fingers. "Just like that. And they got away with it."

Bethany rose stiffly, stumbling. "So, now you think it wasn't an accident? You're just humoring me." It was hard to form the words. She was so cold.

"If you believe it, I believe it. I owe you that," said Tillie.

Bethany's joints ached. She looked at Tillie, her eyes trying to focus. What was that snapping sound? Oh. Her teeth, chattering from the cold. She looked around her, massaging the crimp out of her neck with numb fingers. What was she doing out here? This was so stupid. "They didn't get away with it," she answered, stamping her feet to get the circulation going. "Not by a long shot. Not while I'm still breathing."

She turned around to say goodbye to her mother, to lay her cold hand upon the rough stone, and realized that she was standing on Joe's grave. How on earth could she have gotten them confused?

"Ramona is making a poultice for your chest. You look like an ice queen! Here. Drink this!" she said, shoving an evil-smelling mug under Bethany's nose.

Bethany sat shivering at the counter that divided the tiny kitchen from the living room, wrapped in her trusty quilt. "Absolutely not!" she said, her hands shaking so hard she slopped some of the gross stuff on her quilt.

"Drink it or Ramona will sit on you and pour it down your throat. If your father finds out about this, *mon cherie*, I will surely be fired and then you," she pressed a finger on Bethany's nose, squashing it, "will have to go live with him in New York City. Drink or prepare to move!"

Bethany made a concerted effort to control the tremors in her hands and took a sip. "Yuck!"

"Don't you dare spit it out!" cried Ramona.

"What is this stuff?"

"Yarrow tea. The best for people coming down with a cold or the flu. Now. Drink up!"

"I am not coming down with the flu!"

"Drink!" commanded Ramona.

Bethany cowered in her quilt, then held her nose and started to drink. Cat urine would taste better.

Tillie, perched on the stool beside her, swung her long dark legs lazily back and forth. "Remind me not to be sick around Ramona," she whispered as the housekeeper began humming while she stirred the junk on the stove.

Bethany took an awful sip from the mug. "Has anyone heard from Nick?"

Tillie shook her head. "We think he might have left with Karen's family."

Bethany spit out the tea. "What? And not even attend his sister's funeral? Who will make the arrangements?"

"He called my father this morning and asked if he would handle it for him. Said he just couldn't deal. My mother happened to be at the grocery store across the street from the trailer park around the same time. She saw Nick following Karen's parents in his truck. Karen was in the front seat with him."

"I've been cheated on and dumped," said Bethany. "Life couldn't get much worse."

"Your life won't be worth living if your father finds out you spent hours hugging a gravestone!" said Ramona.

"I wasn't hugging a gravestone. Besides, who's gonna tell him?" asked Bethany, shooting her a dirty look.

Ramona made the sign of the cross and turned back to the stove.

"Look at the bright side," said Tillie. "After I punched Vanessa in the nose, she and her friends asked me to come to their Halloween party at the end of the month and read their cards."

Bethany snorted. "You, who preached nonviolence? What got into you?"

Tillie bit her lip, looking hesitantly at Ramona. "Vanessa also said she's sorry that you got hit on the head. They didn't mean to. They were only going to start a fire on your lawn to scare Bethany's dad into moving away, but when they saw you coming out,

Todd Lancaster threw the gas can and it hit you in the head. She confessed to her parents. They took her car away for the whole year. She says I'm to tell you that you can press charges, if you want. Her parents haven't told the police yet." She turned to Bethany. "She says she'll also replace your backpack."

"She did that, too?" exclaimed Bethany. "But why?"

"She said that she was jealous of you. You've got money, you have a lot of freedom, you always get distinguished honors in school and you're the star of the hockey team, yet you act like . . . well . . . it's no big deal. So, when Karen started to tell her all those lies, she was more than willing to believe them. She wanted you to be bad."

"How horrible," whispered Bethany. "But that's all so ridiculous."

"Ramona will think about calling the police," said Ramona. "What they did was a very dangerous thing. Not only could Ramona have been killed, but they could have been hurt, too." She rubbed her hands. "Perhaps Ramona can think up something else. Like housecleaning and lawn work for a year."

"Press charges," mumbled Bethany. "Daddy will be furious."

Tillie stopped swinging her legs, a meek expression on her face.

"You know," said Bethany, finishing off the last of the noxious tea. "We're no closer to the truth than we were a few weeks ago. Someone runs Joe off the road. Nobody knows why. Marissa kills herself. Nobody knows why. Rather than getting clarity about anything, everything is muddier than before. I really thought that Karen might be the key."

Ramona turned, yellow goo dripping off a wooden spoon. "Maybe she is," said Ramona.

"What do you mean?" asked Tillie.

"Perhaps that is why her parents took her away," remarked Ramona.

Tillie snorted. "Her parents took her away because she's pregnant with Joe's kid."

Ramona shook her head. "Karen is not pregnant."

"Oh, come on, Ramona," said Bethany. "The whole school knows she is pregnant, and I was the last one to find out."

Ramona shook her head. "Not pregnant."

"That's ridiculous," said Tillie, "everyone knows—"

"Knows what?" asked Ramona. "A tale the girl spun? All you have is rumor."

"But she told . . . ," said Tillie, looking guiltily at Bethany.

"Told you. My point," responded Ramona, shaking the wooden spoon coated with yellow junk at her.

Bethany leaned on the counter. "Why would she tell such a drastic lie?"

"I don't know," replied Ramona, "but take this old woman's word for it, the girl is not pregnant."

"How do you know?" asked Tillie.

Ramona shrugged. "I just . . . know." She tapped her head and her heart with her free hand. "I can always tell when a woman is with child. They glow. Karen did not glow. Therefore, Ramona knows she is not going to have a baby."

"But why would Nick go with her?" asked Bethany.

Ramona curled her lip. "How else does one catch a man that has eyes for another?"

"Do you hear that?" asked Tillie, cocking her head.

Bethany coughed. "What?"

"The dogs," said Ramona. "We should call someone to come pick them up. They must belong to someone."

The hair on the back of Bethany's neck stood up as she listened to the keening. Tillie's dark eyes seemed bottomless.

Nervously, Bethany said, "You're not putting that horrid-smelling yellow stuff on my chest."

Ramona faced her, hands on ample hips. "Bet me."

Chapter 20

Saturday, October 3

The radio in Bethany's cherry red Camaro blared the local news, followed by the weather report. A nasty front was headed their way, marching up the coast, then veering west, stomping a path through central Pennsylvania, and was expected to hit their area by nightfall. Bethany flicked the radio off. A storm was a storm was a storm. No biggie.

"Nam is upstairs," said her mother. "I think it's so wonderful that you've offered to take her out for a drive. Be careful, though, she's not supposed to overexert herself. My children should be here by Christmas. Isn't that so exciting?" she said, her delicate lower lip trembling.

Bethany smiled. She was glad something was going right for someone.

The sky had turned from silver to an ominous vomit gray. The girls decided to pick up Tillie, then go to Bethany's house, rather than risk finding themselves on the road in the middle of a storm. They pulled into Bethany's driveway, scattering four huge, black dogs that ran along side the car, growling.

"Do you see them?" she asked Tillie, the hair on her arms standing straight up.

"No, but my mother did. Remember? Do you see them now?" Tillie looked frantically out the windshield.

"I see them," whispered Nam, leaning forward from the backseat. "I never saw such big teeth! Oh, Bethany! What are we going to do? We can't get out of the car with those terrible dogs out there. Who do they belong to?"

Bethany and Tillie exchanged worried glances. Finally, Bethany said, "They don't belong to anybody living . . . they're the Hounds of the Wild Hunt."

Nam's face paled, matching her silver coat. "Those dogs we called? What are they doing here?"

"Guess they can't find the killer either," said Tillie. "How lucky for us."

Ramona appeared at the front door.

She looked again.

No dogs.

"They're, they're gone," Nam whispered from behind silver fingernails. "I bet Ramona scared them off!"

Ramona did not look happy. "*Betes!* Beasts. Ramona sees these big beasts all the time. Why are they here? Who do they belong to?" She gazed pointedly at Bethany, who quickly looked away. Nam and Tillie shifted nervously on the front porch. When no one answered her, Ramona hustled Nam into the house, following the girl like a mother alligator monitoring its young. Bethany and Tillie followed mutely.

"Ramona has done something special for Bethany," she said, dragging the girls into Carl Salem's den, except it wasn't his den anymore. It had become Bethany's bedroom.

"How did you move all my stuff? *Why* did you move all my stuff?" exclaimed Bethany, awed at the beautiful changes in the room.

Ramona smiled. "Bad energies in your room because of the suicide. I cleared out the room with the elements and sent the negativity on its way, but Bethany's memories will stay with her. So," she thrust out her white clad arm with a flourish, "*Voilá! I switched rooms!* I called in a moving company and they were quite happy to do it. They really liked Ramona's cookies. This room is much nicer! See? Northern exposure! Everything comes from the north, you know."

The three girls admired Ramona's handiwork. Not only had she switched the furniture, but there were various prints of Goddesses hanging on the wall.

"My father will be furious," remarked Bethany.

"Not at all, *mon cherie,*" responded Ramona. "Ramona got his permission before she redecorated."

"He agreed?" asked Bethany.

Ramona smiled. "Ramona usually gets what Ramona wants."

"I don't know what to say," said Bethany. "I guess

thank you would be a good start."

Ramona bowed slightly. She straightened, sniffing the air. "My pot roast!" she exclaimed, hurrying out of the room.

"Oh, look there!" said Nam, pointing to one of the pictures. "Kuan Yin! My favorite! My grandfather just sent me a statue of her. I've been trying to incorporate her into my studies!" She turned to Bethany and whispered, "Do you think that's okay?"

"I think that if She pleases you, you should be able to add whatever you want," said Bethany, sitting down on the edge of the bed. "That's the nice thing about Witchcraft. There are moral rules, but no one can tell you who or what to worship, or even how to honor your beliefs. That's why I like it."

"Me too," said Tillie, flopping down on the bed. "I use Oshun as my primary Goddess. She's of Yoruban descent and is the Goddess of lakes, rivers, and streams. She's also the Goddess of gold!" She laughed, twirling a set of tinkling gold bracelets on her wrist. "She's that one, over there."

Nam sat gingerly on the bed. She didn't look too bad. A little washed out, with dark smudges under her eyes, but there was a lot of vitality dancing in her smile. "I have to stay home from school for another week," she said, sighing. "But it isn't too bad. Vanessa Peters called to say she was sorry about the accident and spreading rumors about us. She told me about Karen leaving town. It's all over school that Nick left with her and that she's pregnant with Joe's baby. Is that true?"

Bethany shrugged. "Ramona says not, but Karen claims that she is, and that's what she told Nick. A tinge of sadness tugged at her heart.

Tillie said, "Too true."

"I had no idea, but Vanessa Peters was real informative!" Nam shook her head, her midnight-dark hair dancing around her slender shoulders.

Tillie shifted uncomfortably. Bethany just raised and lowered her eyebrows, her fingers running along the chain of her pentacle necklace.

Nam's eyes watched the backward and forward movement of Bethany's fingers. "You didn't know, did you, Bethany? I'm so sorry."

Tillie said, "Bethany? Does Ramona have any cookies?"

Nam giggled. "Don't you ever stop thinking of food? I don't know how you can eat so much junk and stay so skinny. The rest of us have to diet like crazy. Of course, being in the hospital, I think I lost about ten pounds."

Ramona appeared at the doorway. "Pot roast is fine. Ramona is going over to her apartment to read for awhile. Ramona is reading a book by Lois Duncan. She's right at the good part, so don't bother Ramona, okay?"

"No problem," replied Bethany.

"Oh, and add a little water to the pot roast in half an hour, will you? Ramona doesn't want it to burn." The housekeeper quietly shut the door.

"She said she gave the moving people cookies," said Tillie, her eyes lighting. "I hope they didn't hog them all up." She hurried off to the kitchen in search of the tasty confection, returning a few minutes later with the leering pig cookie jar under one arm, a big smile on her face. "Peanut butter!" she announced.

Bethany turned to Nam. "I just don't get any of this," said Bethany. "I thought maybe it was someone at school, like Vanessa and her friends, but I don't think so. They're just a bunch of kids who listened to Karen's lies. This is so confusing!"

"Maybe they confessed to the lesser things to get away with a bigger crime," suggested Nam.

"You know," said Tillie, fishing for her second cookie, "I think that Paul Neri knows more about all of this than he's letting on."

"You mean that reporter guy?" asked Bethany. "If he knew something, why hasn't he gone to the cops?"

"Like the man said," remarked Tillie. "He needs proof." She bit into the cookie, smacking her lips.

"Lucky for us or he'd have us all carted away. He thinks we did it," said Bethany.

Nam shuddered. "He's the man who saw my accident," said Nam. "That's how they found Marissa's car."

"I didn't know that!" exclaimed Bethany. "You know, the more I think about it, the more I believe he has pieces, but not the full picture. He knew Joe," said Bethany slowly. "And he's been following us around. I think it's time we set a trap for little Paul Neri."

"How do we do that? We don't even know where he's staying!" said Tillie.

"We don't have to know," said Bethany, producing a black ribbon and two red figure candles from her dresser drawer—one male, one female. "He'll come to me."

Nam jumped up. "Where did you get those?"

"An occult shop in New York City over the summer," replied Bethany. "I stayed for a week or two at my dad's apartment. It was easy to sneak out and go to all the stores. I got lots of stuff."

Tillie's dark eyes widened in fear. "I don't know, Bethany. What you want to do is awfully dangerous. You're messing with another person's free will if you're going to do what I think you are."

Bethany straightened. "So?"

"But that's wrong," said Nam.

"And killing Joe was right?"

Tillie folded her arms across the cookie jar, hugging the leering ceramic creature to her chest. "For the thousandth time, we don't know that Joe's death wasn't an accident. You could be putting Neri in danger, let alone yourself."

"The truth shall set you free!" declared Bethany. "And that's how I'll do it. I'll focus on the truth rather than on a particular person. How's that?"

"This could get you killed," mumbled Tillie. "I don't like it." She jerked her arm, the gold bracelets tinkling in the silence of the room.

Nam ran her fingers through her hair, the dark strands falling through her pale, slender fingers like black water, her expression pensive.

Bethany set the candles on her dresser, tying them together with the black cord. "When I get my answers, I'll cut him loose," said Bethany. She began humming, the way her mother taught her. The light in the room appeared to retreat into the corners, dimming softly, as if a black blanket had been thrown across the window.

Bethany slowly raised her arms over her head, visualizing the hedge-circle of old. "I conjure thee, O circle of power," she whispered, "so that you will be for me a boundary between the worlds of men and the realms of the mighty Spirits!"

Her voice gained momentum. "A meeting place of perfect love, trust, peace, and joy, containing the power I will raise herein. I call upon the north, the east, the south, and the west to aid me in this consecration. Thus in the name of the Great Lady, I conjure thee, O great circle of power!" she commanded loudly.

She could hear the hoarse breathing of Tillie behind her and the rapid kitten breaths of Nam. She held her hands over the candles, asking the Great Mother to instill the candles with power and to connect the male to Paul Neri and the female to herself.

Her hands grew hot, and the candles seemed to glow with a blue-violet aura of their own.

"You didn't get this spell out of any book," whispered Tillie. "Where did you get it?" Her gold bracelets clanged with the sudden movement of her arms. "My grandmother taught my mom how to do this!"

Bethany ignored Tillie, continuing to concentrate on the candles. "I call for truth. I call for clarity. I call for justice! Bind this man to me until the truth is revealed!"

"This is a very bad idea," muttered Tillie.

Slowly, Bethany withdrew a lighter from her pocket and set flame first to the male candle, and then to her own. A thunderclap hit the house full force, windows and knickknacks shaking. The picture of Joe bounced from the edge of the dresser, crashing in pieces as it struck the hardwood floor.

The storm that had threatened to engulf Cedar Crest hit with full force.

And Bethany smiled.

She turned slowly, feeling the power surging through her. "My mother taught me," she said, feeling the energy, like an electric shock, playing across her arms, encompassing her head, shooting from her eyes.

Nam screamed.

Tillie just stared at her. "Holy crap," she whispered, then dropped her eyes to the floor. "Hey, hey, look here!" Tillie picked through the broken frame and glass.

The other two girls gathered around Tillie. "Look at this," she said, her voice strangled, her gold bracelets tinkling down her arm mixing with the sonorous chimes of the clock in the hall.

Chapter 21

What is it?" whispered Nam, cringing fearfully as lightening lit up the window and a big boom of thunder rocked the house for a second time. The flash lit up the silver barrettes in her blue-black hair.

"Some sort of . . . hey!" said Tillie, unfurling the papers. "Looks like legal stuff. Maybe a will." Tillie read quickly. "There's two wills here!"

Nam's face grew paler then before. "Why would Joe have put a will behind his picture?"

"Why indeed?" came a fourth voice from the doorway.

The girls whirled. Angela! What was she doing here?

Another crack of lightning. A peal of thunder. The howl of a dog.

"What happened to your face?" asked Tillie.

Angela's hand flew to her cheek. "It's a wart. I'm getting it removed tomorrow. What business is that of yours?"

Tillie snickered, the golden bracelets on her arms laughing with her. "Toadsville," she snickered. "Looks like your spell worked, Nam! She's got a wart on her face the size of a Ping-Pong ball!"

Angela stepped forward gracefully on spiked heels, her manicured hand outstretched. "Give me that!" she spat, waving those long fingers at the papers Tillie held.

Tillie danced back from Angela's fingertips, still reading the papers. She looked up slowly, realization dawning in her dark eyes with an eerie plum light. The papers rattled in Tillie's shaking hands, her bracelets tinkling weakly. Tillie looked up from reading one of the documents. "You killed them," she breathed.

"Don't be absurd! Killed who?" asked Angela, lithely gliding toward Tillie, one hand self-consciously covering her cheek. "Hand those papers over! They are legal documents."

"Yeah," said Tillie, shoving them behind her back, her bracelets whispering against her clothing. "Legal documents signed by you! How did Joe get them?"

"Where's my father?" interrupted Bethany. It was as if she was seeing Angela for the first time. Ramona was right, there seemed to be a black, oozing sheen around the woman. She drew her breath in suddenly. Angela was magickal! She didn't know it (thank the Goddess for small favors) but somewhere within her family history, there'd been a very powerful individual indeed. Bethany's heart tried to jackhammer out of her chest.

"He's in New York, where he should be," announced Angela, her gold earrings glittering as she turned her head. She dangled the house keys in front of the girls. "The door's open downstairs. We're ready to go. Your father and I have decided that it's time to put you away . . . so to speak. I'm taking you to Savannah's Girls' School in upstate New York. Very posh place—for the criminally insane. Of course, your father thinks that it's a boarding school. I let him go about that absurd business of redecorating his den for your new room to keep him thinking you're important—which we both know, you're the last thing I care about! Doesn't matter, though, because he and I are leaving for Europe at the end of the week. By the time your father figures out where you are, you'll be pumped with enough drugs to make you crazy. I'm firing Ramona. Pack your bags." She stepped forward and snatched the papers from Tillie. "Get out and take your sniveling little friend with you."

"We'll tell our parents. We'll tell them you killed Joe!" said Nam, bravely moving closer to Bethany, clutching her coven necklace in her fingers, her silver fingernail polish winking in the bedroom light.

Angela laughed, a high-pitched nasal sound. "As if they'd believe two little teenagers. Poor Bethany has been whirling around for three months trying to sell the murder idea to anyone who would listen. Nobody did. Not even her own father. Go tell anyone you want. The burden of proof lies with you, and you don't have any!"

"How did you get in here?" asked Bethany, remembering the security system.

"Get real. I am your father's girlfriend. He gave me the code. I disabled it. Now get moving!"

Rain lashed at the windows of the bedroom, the sky beyond boiling, the trees bending in the fury of the wind. Something banged against the side of the house. A horrid howling sound emanated from beneath the windows.

Another.

And then another, as if something or someone was trying to break through the walls to get in.

Black forms flew against the window, then fell to the ground. The lights flickered, but remained on.

Quiet.

The girls didn't move.

Angela didn't seem to notice. She tapped the shiny toe of her black high heel impatiently.

"My father would never allow you to take me anywhere without saying goodbye," said Bethany, squaring her shoulders.

"Don't you get it yet, little girl?" said Angela, her eyes carrying an unholy light. "He'll do *anything* I say!"

Bethany's confidence started to drain. "You bewitched him!"

Angela laughed. "You and your stupid magickal beliefs. It's all hogwash. I don't need stupid love spells, honey, I'm just *real* good at what I do."

Bethany watched the blackness grow around Angela . . . she remembered what Ramona had said, "Some people come into this world with the power, but never realize it . . ."

"I'm not leaving," said Bethany. "You can't *make* me go anywhere with you."

Whereupon Angela unceremoniously produced a gun from the pocket of her black blazer and aimed it at Nam. "I thought this might happen if your little cronies were with you. I'd hoped you would be alone. However, I came prepared. Either you pack your bags or this one meets that fake Goddess you're so proud of."

"You'd never shoot her," said Tillie. "Then it would all come tumbling down."

Angela waved the gun in the air. "I'll just tell her father that it was a teen cult thing. He'll believe me."

Bethany didn't like the savagery she heard in the woman's voice. She realized with cold logic that the moment Angela saw Tillie with those papers she never intended to let any of them out of here alive. She'd come *prepared* to kill—except she thought that Bethany and Ramona would be here, not Bethany's friends.

Simple as that.

Bethany began concentrating, gathering her anger, remembering what happened to Mrs. Matthews. She did it once by accident, could she do it again on purpose? She could feel the power gathering within her, but could she conjure it fast enough? She grabbed Tillie and Nam's hands. "We are the weavers, we are the web," she said, looking at the other two girls. "We are the Witches, back from the dead!"

The other girls took up the chant, Tillie moving her arm, the golden bracelets tinkling to the beat.

Tillie closed her eyes.

Nam stared hard at the ceiling, the silver lipstick on her mouth gleaming.

They chanted louder.

Only Bethany looked at Angela straight in the eyes, daring her to pull the trigger.

The still point.

Bethany opened her mind and seized it.

Again, the howling from beneath the window. This time, Angela heard it. The gun tremored slightly. The girls continued to chant. Angela's eyes flicked nervously around the room. "Stop it!" she screamed. "Stop it!" Her finger moved on the trigger.

"Well, if this isn't an interesting moment, and here's the biggest Witch of them all, holding a gun on a bunch of defenseless little Witches," came a male voice from behind Angela. She whirled, facing Paul Neri, the pesky but dogged reporter. Leave your door open and anything might slither in. The flash mechanism on his camera filled the room with a piercing knife of pulsing light. "Snooping pays off!" he cried.

"You!" screeched Angela.

Hecate streaked through Paul's legs, barreling straight for Angela, four massive black dogs hot on the cat's heels. Neri flew up in the air and back-wards, his camera soaring through the hallway, smashing into the hall clock. The mechanism uttered a sickening chime.

Angela screamed.

Neri hit the floor, flat on his back, cracking his head on the hardwood floor.

Hecate's claws sunk into the flesh of Angela's calves, his fur nothing put a huge black puff.

Angela's gun hand flew straight up, the blast of two shots hitting the ceiling, bits of plaster raining down. Tillie and Nam dove to the side as the dogs soared through the air, filling the room with a heavy canine odor, knocking Angela to the hardwood floor, powerful jaws munching through her skin like a laser obliterating a piece of paper.

Hecate howled, springing from the floor to the dresser, knocking over the two burning candles, raining hot wax and fire on Angela's head. The two candles broke apart, sputtered, and went out.

The crazed woman raised the gun and aimed for Tillie's head, the shot echoing through the room as one of the dogs tore her arm from her shoulder.

The sound of golden bracelets hitting the hardwood floor.

Screams sending shock waves through Bethany's body.

Angela was dead.

There were pieces of her everywhere. Just like Nam had wished.

Just like Joe.

Bethany looked at her left hand, expecting to be

holding on to a dead Tillie.

But Tillie wasn't there.

Nam collapsed on the floor, crying, her black hair cascading around her face like a stormy wet cloud. Paul Neri, flat on his back, did not move. He was out cold, and his camera was in pieces, strewn across the hallway.

His career was getting mighty expensive.

Bethany stood in the center of the room, a tiny thought echoing in her mind as she looked at the upside-down alarm clock on her dresser. It was exactly one month, to the minute, that they'd first done the ritual to catch Joe's killer.

Bethany sank slowly to the bloody floor. Thunder boomed in the distance.

I guess the magick worked, she thought shakily.

But at what deadly cost?

"Tillie?" she screamed. "O my Goddess! Tillie!"

Chapter 22

Ramona sat at the dining room table, braiding Bethany's hair into one long, heavy plait. "Look at how much your hair has grown," she mused. "See, trimming it only on the full moon really does help your hair grow."

"What else are you putting in my hair?" asked Bethany, looking at a pile of brightly colored ribbons and little trinkets spread on the dining room table amongst various other clutter.

Ramona didn't answer. Hecate sat atop a stack of papers on the table, pawing at a silver bell.

Bethany shifted on the chair. "So what *are* you putting in my hair?"

"Why, Ramona is weaving in orange for vitality, black for protection, and bells to break any negativity."

"I'm going to look stupid at the Halloween party," said Bethany sourly.

"You are not!" exclaimed Ramona. "Everyone will love you! You'll be the prettiest Witch there."

"You're weaving in a glamoury, aren't you?"

"And what if I am? It certainly helped Tillie! She dodged that bullet and only got grazed. How is *your* practice coming?"

Bethany gagged. As if school wasn't enough, now she was studying under Ramona. Nam and Tillie, too.

Tillie was doing just fine. She'd used Ramona's spell for stopping gossip just the other night. Now the three of them had been invited to Vanessa's Halloween party, which wasn't exactly what they'd anticipated, but it might be fun. Everybody who was cool would be there.

Bethany tried to quell her excitement. Her stomach felt jittery. She'd never been invited to a party thrown by a member of the popular crowd. What if she screwed up?

A loud tumble of stainless steel cookware crashing about the kitchen made her jump, jerking her hair from Ramona's hands. "What's that?" she yipped.

"Your father, wrestling with the meatloaf. He said that since I was helping you get ready for the party, he would make the dinner. Ramona thinks this is a big mistake, but I'm only the keeper, *mon cherie.*" She winked. "Sit still, will you?" complained Ramona. "This won't come out right if you continue to squirm!"

"Ouch!" Bethany frowned, gazing out the picture window. Her fingers strayed to her coven necklace, the one with the pentacle and eight phases of the moon. The circular disk tingled at the gentle touch of her fingers. Large golden leaves, as big as a dog's paw, drifted past the window, dipping softly to the ground.

Dog. She shivered. But there were no dogs. At least, that's what her father had said. And there was no blood. And Angela wasn't in pieces on the floor. They'd claimed that the Beast of the East had died of a myocardial infarction—heart attack. Odd, for a woman her age, but not unheard of. Ramona explained that sometimes we see things on the astral for real, and on the earth plane as illusion, especially when magick is involved. It's rare, but it happens.

Paul Neri didn't see the dogs because the fall knocked him out. When he came to, the paramedics and the cops were there. Neri sold his story for a few hundred grand to a trash paper, capitalizing on the woman-killer dogs he'd never seen. So much for investigative journalism. At least he could buy himself a new camera.

Bethany drew her breath in sharply as Ramona pulled too hard. "Hey!" she exclaimed. "Easy!" Her hand strayed to a post card on the table depicting sunny Florida, with white beaches and palm trees and one of those stupid "wish you were here" messages. She flipped the card over, rereading it for the hundredth time: *Bethany, Karen and I are doing well. I'm living with her parents for now. No baby, but that's okay, we want to finish school before we start a family. We found a circle here in Tampa, but not half as good as WNO. Love, Nick.*

Unbelievable. Why did they take off in the first place? Perhaps that was a mystery Bethany would never unravel, and at this point, she really didn't care any more. *They say there is no sanity in love or war,* she thought, *and perhaps they're right, whoever they are.*

Ramona hummed, her dark, nimble fingers working through Bethany's heavy hair.

It took several days for Bethany's father to unwind the tangled details of the whole mess. It was a racket. Angela's racket. She lured in mentally unstable rich people, like Marissa, convinced them to off their parents, and then collected huge amounts of money, first for helping the relative to set up the murder, and then cashing in on a blackmail scheme. If they got too mouthy, or too crazy, Angela arranged for them to disappear: some of them to the Savannah Clinic in upper New York, others in the middle of Lake Erie. There really was a conspiracy. Poor Marissa.

Angela never worked twice in the same town, and she always dated someone from the local law to cover the swindle. Cedar Crest, though, had no available officers, with a force of eight and all of them married. Angela scouted for something close and found an unexpected bonus—Carl Salem and his marvelous money.

Bethany's father thought that Marissa originally dragged Joe into the fray. It was his supposition that Marissa broke down and told Joe in an effort to keep him tied to her, thinking that if he knew of the crime, he was just as guilty.

According to a sobbing Karen, hauled in for

questioning twenty-four hours after Angela's death, Joe had been seeing quite a few girls, including Vanessa Peters, Karen, and Marissa. Karen originally wanted to leave Witches' Night Out first because she was afraid that if the truth around Joe's death came out, the truth of other things would follow. She truly believed that Joe's accident was just that—a fateful flip of the coin of life and death—but she also knew that when one works a spell for truth, one should be ready for the consequences if your own slate isn't clean. The more she thought about it, the more she feared that Nick would discover her past involvement with Joe. The march of lies spewing from her mouth began, and the more she fibbed the worse it got.

Bethany's father also believed that Joe confronted Angela the night of his death. Carl Salem wasn't clear on why Joe hadn't gone to the police, but Bethany thought she knew the answer.

Before meeting Angela, Joe placed the two wills belonging to Marissa's parents behind his picture, at least proving he wasn't stupid. Perhaps he thought to blackmail the woman. The real will cut Marissa out of her inheritance due to her parents' exasperation with her insane lifestyle. The second, the one used at the time the estate was settled, was a fraud.

Had Joe given the wills to Bethany hoping that if anything happened, she would figure it out?

How considerate of him.

It wasn't Bethany who grasped the purpose of the

wills, but Tillie did. That psychism and common sense of hers melded at the right time, not necessarily the right place. That girl was definitely fey.

Ramona jerked Bethany's hair. "Hey! Stop woolgathering. Did you hear me?"

Bethany shook her head as much as Ramona's strong grip would allow. "What?"

"I need more of those small rubber bands."

"I have some," said Bethany, stretching the kinks out of her back as she rose, the black satin of her Witch costume rustling as she raised her arms. She flexed her fingers. Hecate continued to bat the bell until it fell on the floor, scattering the pile of papers he was using for a perch. "What's this?" she asked, picking up the papers.

"A case your father is working on. The one with the little girl," said Ramona.

"You mean he *still* hasn't solved it yet?"

Ramona nodded her head sadly.

Bethany swallowed hard, putting the papers in the folder. Something, she wasn't sure what, wafted through her mind.

She quickly went to her room and opened her dresser drawer, rummaging for the rubber bands. Her hands brushed across the loose picture of Joe, lost under a pile of blue ribbons from various athletic completions, a half-empty Chapstick container, and a hockey puck.

She raised the picture slowly, feeling a rush of jumbled emotions. She'd found his killer. Could she do a repeat performance? Could she discover who murdered the little girl?

Why not?

Let's see, Witches' Night Out was next Thursday . . .

She gazed at the picture again, now torn in some places, a crack running across Joe's handsome, smiling face, reminding her of that disgusting cookie jar in the kitchen.

Bethany turned to see Hecate's dark form poised in the open doorway, head cocked slightly, eyes bright and feral. She shivered. "Guess you're a real familiar, after all."

She looked down at the picture and crumpled the smiling face of Joe with both hands, exorcising him from her heart.

And just for a moment . . .

The briefest second . . .

She thought she heard someone whisper in her ear, "Who loves ya, baby?"

Epilogue

Ramona's Spell for Stopping Gossip

Although this story about Bethany and her friends is a work of fiction, magick and the religion of Wicca is very real. Today, Witchcraft is the fastest growing religion in the United States. The religion's earth-centered appeal and its premise that all are equal regardless of race, religion, income bracket, or sexual preference, combined with its teachings that everyone has personal power and the ability to achieve whatever he or she desires in a positive way, has rocketed the Old Religion to new heights. And, of course, there's always the magick . . .

A spell is simply a focused prayer often using material things to help the mind concentrate on the issue at hand. This particular spell is approximately 300 years old, and originates from Germany. To stop harmful gossip, you will need a potato, a black marker, black pepper, and a ladies' hair net (you can get the hair net at the grocery store for about a dollar). Write the person's name who is talking about you on the potato with the black marker. Cut a small hole in the potato and fill it with black pepper (for banishing). Wrap the potato in the hair net. Tie the ends securely, concentrating on the gossip leaving your life. Bury off your property. As you put the last bit of dirt over the potato, say the following charm:

> Three ladies came from the east
> Bringing frost and fire
> One said, "I silence thee."
> The second said, "I banish thee."
> The third sunk them in the mire.
> So mote it be!

Say the charm three times, then make the sign of an equal-armed cross over the buried potato to seal the magick. Say nothing to anyone—enchantments should be private. This spell works best if done over the full moon, or when the moon is dark.

National Hotlines

The following numbers were collected by a Pennsylvania sheriff (a friend of mine) in case you ever need them. Don't be shy. If you need help, please call. If you have to do a report in school on any of the issues listed below, the people at these numbers will be happy to supply you information.

Alcohol and Drug Abuse

Al-Anon & Alateen: 1-800-356-9996

National Clearinghouse for Alcohol & Drug Information: 1-800-SAY-NOTO

National Cocaine Hotline: 1-800-262-2463

Alcohol & Drug Dependency Hopeline: 1-800-622-2255

National Institute on Drug Abuse Hotline: 1-800-622-HELP

Mothers Against Drunk Driving: 1-800-438-MADD

Abuse

Bureau of Indian Affairs Child Abuse Hotline: 1-800-633-5133

Boy's Town: 1-800-448-3000

Child Help USA: 1-800-422-4453

National Respite Locaters Service: 1-800-773-5433

National Domestic Violence Hotline:
   1-800-799-7233

National Clearinghouse of Child Abuse and
   Neglect: 1-800-394-3366

National Resource Center on Domestic Violence:
   1-800-553-2508

Rape, Abuse & Incest National Network:
   1-800-656-4673

Resource Center on Domestic Violence, Child
   Protection and Custody: 1-800-527-3223

Runaways Hotlines

Covenant House Nineline: 1-800-999-9999

National Runaway Switchboard: 1-800-621-4000

National Child Welfare

Child Find of America: 1-800-I-AM-LOST

Child Quest International Sighting Line:
   1-800-248-8020

National Referral Network for Kids in Crisis:
   1-800-KID-SAVE

Health & AIDS/HIV

AIDS Helpline: 1-800-548-4659

Ask A Nurse Connection: 1-800-535-1111

National AIDS Hotline: 1-800-342-AIDS

STD National Hotline: 1-800-227-8922

About Silver

Silver RavenWolf is the author of over thirteen how-to and fictional books relating to the application of the magickal sciences. She resides in south-central Pennsylvania with her husband of twenty-one years, four children, sheltie, and pet rat. Her primary interests are divinatory tools, astrology, hypnotherapy, reading, swimming, and getting through life in a positive and productive way. To read about Silver, her touring schedule, upcoming events, and books, visit Silver's website at:

http://www.silverravenwolf.com

To Write to Silver

If you wish to contact the author or would like more information about this book, please write to:

Silver RavenWolf
℅ Llewellyn Worldwide
P.O. Box 64383, Dept. K728-5
St. Paul, MN 55164-0383, U.S.A.

Please enclose a self-addressed stamped envelope for reply,
or $1.00 to cover costs. If outside U.S.A.,
enclose international postal reply coupon.

About the Series

In September of 1998 my book entitled *Teen Witch* was published, shocking myself and the publishing world with phenomenal sales. I wrote the book because I cared about kids and I wanted them to have legitimate information on how to work real magick. I hung the rave reviews and the advertising poster given to me by Llewellyn above my desk. For me, it was a dream come true. I'd written a book that would make a difference in people's lives. While working on other projects, I would stare at that poster, thinking about the thousands of teens reading my book.

One afternoon, my sixteen-year-old daughter, Falcon, caught me at my desk once again mesmerized by that poster. "Too bad those kids on the cover of your book aren't real," she said. "I mean, they look like real people, don't they?"

The hairs on the back of my neck stood up as I continued to look at the poster. "Yeah," I breathed. "I've stared at this picture so long, they *do* seem like they are more than just a book cover. It's like . . . I don't know . . . as if I've known them all along. That one's Bethany," I said, pointing to the dark-haired girl in the center of the picture. "And I think the

African-American girl looks just like a Tillie. What do you think?"

Falcon surveyed the poster, then turned to me with a sly smile. "You know, Echo is always complaining that you never wrote fiction for us." Echo is Falcon's older sister. "Why don't you write a story about the kids on the poster?"

And that's how the Witches' Night Out series was born. Although the story is entirely fictional, I set about to devise a world where the teens use real magick, not the fairy tale stuff. It wasn't easy. In the world of fiction, anything can happen. It would have been so easy to give Bethany and her friends superpowers, but I know that real magick doesn't work that way. Conjuring magick is a skill that one acquires after hard work and practice. It takes longer than a snap of your fingers, and it almost never happens with the bells and whistles of a Hollywood film—but it does happen. Bethany and her friends are students of magick, which in a way makes it all the more fun! They will make mistakes as they wrestle with school, family problems, and relationships with peers—not to mention the pain of dealing with a job at the same time, an already rocky road for any kid. Throw in the desire to solve crimes, and the characters become people like you are me. That's why their world is such an interesting one!

Because . . . it *could* be real.

**Teen Witch Kit:
Everything You Need
to Make Magick!**

Silver RavenWolf

Here is everything the novice spell-caster needs to practice the Craft of The Wise—and be a force for good. Step into the sacred space and discover the secrets of one of the world's oldest mysteries: the art and science of white magick, a gentle, loving practice. The kit contains a beautifully illustrated book of instruction, plus six magickal talismans, salt, and a spell bag. The kit box converts into your own personal altar.

Silver RavenWolf, one of today's most famous Witches and author of the best-selling *Teen Witch*, provides the quick-reading guidebook, complete with instructions on how to prepare yourself for magick, create a sacred space, call up the spirit, and draw down the Moon.

All the spells are tailored to 13- to 18-year olds, and can be cast using the items in the kit and common objects found around the house. It's easy to follow the step-by-step instructions and clear magickal symbols. There is even a section on how to write your own spells. The book also reveals the white magick code of honor, and includes a glossary of terms, a suggested reading list, and a guide to the top magickal Internet sites.

1-56718-554-1 $24.95
7½ x 7½ boxed kit contains:
  128-pp. illus. book • spell bag • spell salt • golden coin • silver wish cord • silver bell • natural quartz crystal • silver pentacle pendant • yes/no coin

Teen Witch: Wicca for a New Generation

Silver RavenWolf

Teenagers and young adults comprise a growing market for books on Witchcraft and magick, yet there has never been a book written specifically for the teen seeker. Now, Silver RavenWolf, one of the most well-known Wiccans today and the mother of four young Witches, gives teens their own handbook on what it takes and what it means to be a Witch. Humorous and compassionate, *Teen Witch* gives practical advice for dealing with everyday life in a magickal way. From homework and crabby teachers to parents and dating, this book guides teens through the ups and downs of life as they move into adulthood. Spells are provided that address their specific concerns, such as the "Call Me Spell" and "The Exam Spell."

Parents will also find this book informative and useful as a discussion tool with their children. Discover the beliefs of Witchcraft, Wiccan traditions, symbols, holidays, rituals, and more.

1-56718-725-0
288 pp., 7 x 10 $12.95